To Find Where She Belongs

THE BRITISH ARE COMING

BOOK FIVE

ROBIN LEE HATCHER

Where She Belongs. From the first page, I was rooting for Keely to step into her happily-ever-after . . . and for William to realize she was the key to his happiness. With relatable characters, tender emotion, and hints of intrigue, Hatcher weaves a story that touches the heart and reminds us of the importance of faith, home, and family. You will love this addition to The British Are Coming Series." — Kim Vogel Sawyer, award-winning author of *Hope's Enduring Echo*

Prologue

New York Harbor
March 1897

Keely Boyle stood at the steamship's railing, gripping the worn wood, the salty wind tugging at her shawl. Damp air carried the scent of coal smoke and brine, but she fixed her attention on the great harbor ahead. Her breath caught as she spotted the towering figure in the distance.

Lady Liberty.

The statue stood resolute against the gray sky, its torch raised high. Keely's pulse quickened at the sight. For eleven miserable days at sea, she'd dreamed of this moment, and now it was here.

America.

Twelve years ago, she'd crossed a much smaller body of water, sailing from Ireland to England. At the age of fifteen, she'd found employment as a housemaid, working in the grand manor of the Earl of Hooke—polishing silver, scrubbing floors, and smoothing linens finer than anything she would ever own. She'd learned to move through the world of the aristocracy with quiet efficiency, never calling attention to herself.

And yet, Roger Bernhardt had noticed her. Dear Roger. He, too, had come from humbler beginnings. Perhaps that was why he'd seen her.

A lump rose in her throat. How foolish she'd been to imagine he might return her affections. He'd been kind, yes. A friend, perhaps. But he'd left England for America nearly two years ago without a backward glance or a second thought. Keely had been left behind, too, still scrubbing floors and polishing silver.

And there she might have stayed forever, if it hadn't been for Mr. Brown, valet to Lord Brandish. Lord and Lady Brandish had come to Hooke Manor for an extended visit, along with many other lords and ladies. Below stairs, Mr. Brown had taken an interest in Keely, always lurking, always watching. She would have sworn she could feel his gaze on her skin. A most unpleasant sensation.

Worse had been the night he'd actually touched her. Not just touched. He'd grabbed her, kissed her, and tried to force himself upon her, his grip bruising her skin. She'd kicked him and slipped from his clutches, but she'd known she wouldn't escape the next time he tried. He would be ready for her. There was evil in him, an evil that would refuse to be denied.

The very next morning, she'd come upon Roger's

letter while cleaning her master's study. Not a letter to Keely, of course. He'd never written to her. It was a letter to the earl and countess. A letter that had accompanied one of his paintings of a place called Eden's Gate Ranch.

She shouldn't have read the letter. It wasn't her place to do so. But she *had* read it, and Roger's words had promised her a better life in a better place, away from the danger that lurked below stairs. And perhaps a life with someone who *saw* her—and cared about her.

She curled her hands into fists to stop their trembling. Soon, she would step onto Ellis Island and tell the officials she had work waiting for her in Idaho, on a ranch called Eden's Gate. She would tell that lie because she had to. She would say whatever she must in order to be admitted to this country. A woman alone, with no employment secured, was too easily turned away. Or so she had been told.

Sweet sufferin' cats! The thought of being turned away sent a chill through her.

A child's voice broke through the murmur of the passengers. "Mama, look! She's smiling at us!"

Keely's gaze flickered back to the statue's face. Smiling? No, the copper lady was solemn, strong. And yet, there was something in her bearing, something steady and unwavering, that made Keely stand a little straighter.

Sure and I did the right thing.

She swallowed hard. She'd wondered often during the voyage if she'd made a mistake. But it was too late to turn back now. Whatever waited for her on the other side of Ellis Island—hardship, uncertainty, and perhaps a new beginning—she would face it.

The ship rocked as it slowed, and a hum of excitement spread through the crowd. They had arrived. Keely squared her shoulders.

Perhaps God would grant her mercy. Even if she was a liar ... and a thief.

Chapter One

Eden's Gate Ranch
March 1897

William Overstreet hunched his shoulders against the icy wind buffeting him as he rode toward the barn at Eden's Gate. Several cowboys followed in his wake, all of them too tired and cold to talk. It was the end of a long day. The calendar might claim it was officially spring, but the temperature said otherwise.

After tending to his horse, he bid good evening to the ranch hands still in the barn, then strode toward the house. He would've welcomed a long soak in a hot bath, but he'd have to make do with a quick wash. Dinner wasn't far off.

He'd come to dread the solitary evenings at the dining room table. He'd never minded being alone in the big house—just him, the housekeeper, and the cook. But frequent, long-term guests over the past couple of years had changed that. After Sebastian, Amanda, and Roger arrived in the spring of '95—followed by Isaiah and Victoria in the months that followed—he'd grown used to lively conversations at breakfast and dinner. Often at both.

There were days he considered joining the boys out in the bunkhouse. Mrs. Adler wouldn't think it right, of course, but the camaraderie might be worth enduring her disapproval.

As he stepped onto the porch, one of the ranch dogs rose to greet him. He patted Old Blue's head, then stomped his boots, hoping to shake off dust and dirt before entering the house. The front door opened, surprising him, and Mrs. Adler appeared.

"Oh, Mr. William. I'm glad you're back at last. There's a woman here to see you, and I wasn't quite sure what to do with her."

What to do with her? He frowned. "I'm sorry, Mrs. Adler?" He gave his head a slow shake, as if that might clear away the confusion.

"She's a stranger to these parts." The housekeeper stood erect, chin high, hands folded neatly in front of her apron. "A foreigner."

He nearly laughed. Now it made sense. Mrs. Adler hadn't been thrilled when Sebastian and the others arrived either. He didn't recall her outright calling them foreigners, but her disapproving manner had been much the same.

"Does this woman have a name?"

"I suppose she does, but she didn't give it to me. She asked if this was the Overstreet ranch, and I said it was.

Then she asked for Mr. Bernhardt, and when I told her he lived in town with his wife, she burst into tears. She has said little since. Just sniffles and shakes her head and mumbles something that sounds like, 'What am I to do?'" Mrs. Adler lowered her voice to a whisper. "She's Irish."

Despite how it sounded, William knew Mrs. Adler didn't bear any real ill will toward people from Ireland. She would sound exactly the same no matter who sat in the Overstreet parlor, sniffling and mumbling.

He swept off his hat and raked a hand through his hair. "I suppose I'd better speak with her before I wash up."

Inside, he placed his hat on the rack in the entry hall, shrugged out of his coat, and hung it beside the hat. Drawing a breath, he turned and walked into the parlor, bracing himself for whatever—or whomever—awaited him.

He wasn't prepared.

The young woman leapt to her feet, looking as frightened as a jackrabbit caught in the open. Her green eyes were wide, her curly red hair wild around her face.

"Miss?"

She clasped her hands. "Would you be Mr. Overstreet?"

"I am."

"Saints be praised." Tears welled in her eyes and slipped down her cheeks.

"I'm sorry, miss. Should I know you?"

"No, sir. But you'd be knowing Mr. Bernhardt. And my master too."

"Your master?"

"Lord Hooke."

He blinked. "Lord Hooke? You mean Sebastian Whitcombe?"

She nodded.

Despite her answers, he felt no less confused than before. He motioned to the settee. "Please have a seat."

She complied at once.

William drew another breath and settled into a chair opposite her. "Let's start again." He touched his chest. "I'm William Overstreet. What's your name?"

"Boyle, sir. Keely Boyle."

"And why have you come to my ranch, Miss Boyle?"

Her complexion paled. "I was hoping to find Mr. Bernhardt. He is . . . he's by way of being a friend of mine."

"A friend?" He sounded like a parrot, repeating everything she said.

"Yes, sir, Mr. Overstreet."

He cleared his throat. "You say you worked for Lord Hooke. What did you do?"

"I was a housemaid, sir."

"When was that?"

"I worked at Hooke Manor for twelve years, I did. First for the old Lord Hooke, then for the new master. I only . . . I left my work there to emigrate to America. Mr. Bernhardt wrote as how he loved his life in America, and the painting he sent made me want to see this country for meself. And so I came straight here."

Confusion returned in full. "Roger sent you a painting?"

Color rose in her cheeks, and her gaze dropped to the floor between them. She mumbled something he couldn't make out.

It wasn't beyond belief that Roger would have corresponded with a maidservant or sent her a painting. He was the sort of man who made friends in both high and low stations. What seemed strange was that this young woman had followed him to America after so much time had passed.

Surely Roger would've stopped writing to Keely Boyle long before he married Victoria.

Another lie.

Sure and she was going to have to tell another one. It already felt to Keely as if she'd lied her way across an ocean. Surprising, really, that she'd made it to this country and this ranch at all, given how poor she was at telling tales. Whenever she fibbed, her cheeks turned red and blotchy, and she couldn't meet anyone's gaze—looking just as guilty as she felt.

Oh, how ashamed her mam would be if she could see her now. The woman had taught her to be honest at all times. Was it possible she could be so again, after all she'd done and said?

Drawing a deep breath, Keely lifted her gaze toward William Overstreet.

"No, sir. Mr. Bernhardt didn't send the painting to

me. It was a gift for Lord and Lady Hooke. But I saw it every time I cleaned the master's study."

He seemed to relax a little at that, and she relaxed, too, grateful for having told the plain truth. It was a start, at least.

"Miss Boyle, I believe my housekeeper mentioned that Mr. Bernhardt no longer resides at my ranch. He lives in Gibeon now. It's a town about six miles from here."

"So she told me."

"It's too late in the day to send word to him about your arrival."

Fear rippled up her spine. She had nowhere to go. Worse still, she had little money left. What had remained of her funds—all but a few dollars—went to hiring a rig and driver to bring her to Eden's Gate Ranch. She'd been so certain she would find refuge with Roger. Convinced he'd be glad to see her, might even realize how much he'd missed their conversations.

"Sweet sufferin' cats," she whispered.

"I'm sorry?"

She shook her head quickly. "'Tis nothing, sir."

"You're welcome to stay here tonight."

"Here?" Her gaze swept over the parlor. She'd worked in a beautiful manor for the past dozen years, but her own quarters had been small and plain, shared with another maid. Was there such a modest room in this house where she could lay her head?

He stood. "Mrs. Adler."

The housekeeper appeared in the doorway almost

instantly, making it clear she'd been listening to every word.

"Take Miss Boyle to a room upstairs and see that she has whatever she needs to be comfortable." He turned back to Keely. "You'll join me for dinner. I'm sure you're hungry after your journey. Mrs. Adler will let you know when it's time. We can talk more then."

Keely was hungry—ravenous, if she were honest— but she couldn't imagine sitting at a table with this man. That wouldn't be proper. Despite the dust on his boots and the worn look of his trousers, his bearing told her he was a gentleman.

"Mr. William—" the housekeeper began.

"I insist," he said. Without another word, he strode from the parlor and disappeared down a hallway at the back of the house.

Mrs. Adler stepped fully into the parlor. "If you'll follow me, miss, I'll show you to your room."

Keely wanted to object. But what good would it do? She didn't know where she was, and even if she did, she had no way to leave. Not that she was afraid of a good long walk, but she'd seen enough of this country to know it might take days to reach another ranch—or the town he'd mentioned. And with nightfall closing in, she'd be lost before the stars came out.

The housekeeper cast a meaningful glance at Keely's valise, then turned and headed for the staircase. Keely retrieved the small suitcase from the corner where she'd dropped it earlier and hurried after her. At the top of the stairs, Mrs. Adler turned left and opened a door a few steps down the hallway.

It took great resolve not to gasp aloud.

The room was truly beautiful. A four-poster bed stood beneath a lace-draped canopy. A large wardrobe of dark polished wood anchored one wall. In the corner, a full-length mirror gleamed near a washbasin, with a window overlooking the vast rangeland.

"I hope this will suit you," Mrs. Adler said.

Suit her? The thought of laying her head there was impossible. She wasn't fit for it. She'd cleaned rooms like this, but she'd never slept in one.

"Sure and I'm thinkin' there must be something less grand where I could stay." Her voice was hushed, almost reverent.

The housekeeper arched an eyebrow. "I assure you, there is not." She pointed down the hall. "The water closet is the third door on the left. Feel free to freshen up. Dinner will be ready in half an hour. I'll come for you then."

"Perhaps I could just get a bite from the kitchen—"

"Mr. William wants you to eat with him." Mrs. Adler turned to leave. "Heaven knows why." She shut the door behind her.

Heaven knew why, indeed.

Chapter Two

Freshly washed and shaved, William ran a comb through his damp hair, the grime of the day now a memory. Moments later, he stepped out of his bedchamber and descended the stairs. It didn't surprise him to find his houseguest already in the dining room.

Keely Boyle stood near the table, her fingers curled around the back of a chair, her teeth worrying her lower lip. She had brushed the dust of travel from her clothing and wrangled her fiery curls into a semblance of order. At the sight of him, she stiffened and then curtsied.

He would've sworn he heard his friend Sebastian laughing somewhere in the back of his mind.

Resisting a grin, William motioned to the chair before her. "Please. Join me."

She hesitated, as if unsure what he meant, then sat, perching on the edge of the seat, stiff-backed and quiet.

"I trust your room is all right," he said.

"'Tis very grand, sir. Too grand for the likes of me, I'm thinking."

"I'd have to disagree. You're a guest in my home, Miss Boyle, which means I want you to have the best I can offer."

"You're too kind, sir."

The door to the kitchen swung open, and Mrs. Adler entered carrying a platter of roast beef. Juices pooled beneath the crusted edges, and the air filled with the mouthwatering scent of garlic, rosemary, and browned onions.

"That smells wonderful, Mrs. Adler."

The housekeeper gave a brisk nod. "It ought to. Chuck had it slow-roasting since midmorning. There's mashed turnips and carrots with butter, and fresh bread still warm from the oven. I'll be back with the rest in a moment." She turned on her heel and disappeared into the kitchen.

Keely's eyes had widened, though she quickly lowered them again.

William bowed his head. "Come, Lord Jesus, be our Guest; and let Thy gifts to us be blessed. Amen."

"Amen," came Keely's soft reply.

He reached for the carving knife and sliced generous portions of meat. "I hope you have a good appetite, Miss Boyle."

"I do, sir. Thank you."

He passed her a plate, then served himself. Mrs. Adler returned with the promised side dishes, set them in place and, with a glance at William, left the room again.

For a moment, only the gentle clink of silverware and china disturbed the quiet.

He saw Keely take a tentative bite of roast. A look of pure pleasure crossed her face. She cut several more bites and ate them quickly, as though the food might vanish if she didn't finish in time.

He didn't know why, but she reminded him of a forest creature—shy, watchful. Or perhaps of a mischievous fairy from one of the fables he'd learned during his time in England. That second thought, he suspected, had more to do with the wild tangle of red curls than anything else. She seemed timid at first glance, but there was strength beneath the surface.

An exquisite surface, he admitted.

He cleared his throat, slightly annoyed at himself. "So, Miss Boyle. You said you worked for the Earl of Hooke."

"Yes, sir. For twelve years."

"You must've started as a young girl."

"I was just fifteen when I arrived in England."

"And why did you leave your homeland?"

"After me mam died when I was fourteen, there wasn't much reason to stay in Ireland." She set her fork on the edge of her plate. "Times were hard, and work was scarce. I had no other family. I hadn't much choice but to leave."

He sensed she was holding something back. Things darker than she wanted to say. "What about your father?"

"Me da died when I was ten."

A pang tugged at William's chest. She'd been making her own way since fourteen. Still little more than a child.

"Mr. Overstreet." She kept her eyes on her plate. "You should know . . . I've little money left. I spent near everything I had just to get here. The ship. The train. Hiring the rig." Her voice faltered. "'Twas pure foolishness, I know that now."

"You believed Mr. Bernhardt could help you."

A flush rose in her cheeks. "So I did. He was always kind when he visited Hooke Manor. I thought . . ." She hesitated, then lifted her gaze. "I thought maybe he'd be glad to see me. Maybe he'd remember our talks." Her voice dropped. "I just needed to leave. Hooke Manor wasn't home. I wanted to begin again. Mr. Bernhardt made Idaho sound so . . . full of hope. In this place, dreams could come true. It was a safe place. A place I could belong."

He heard the catch in her voice as she turned her head away. He wished he could reach across the table, take her hand, offer comfort in some tangible way. But propriety held him in check. Still, he could do something. "Miss Boyle, what would you think of working here? At Eden's Gate. I imagine Mrs. Adler wouldn't mind having some help keeping this place in order."

Her eyes returned to his. "Work here, sir? As a housemaid?"

"Why not?" He warmed to the idea as he said it. "It would give you time to get your bearings, decide whether you want to stay in Idaho or go somewhere else. San Francisco, maybe. Or back east."

"That's kind of you, so it is."

"Not just kind." He emphasized the words with a nod. "Practical. As I said, Mrs. Adler could use an extra pair of hands." He imagined the housekeeper's response to that and almost chuckled. She'd give him an earful later, no doubt.

"And where would I stay, sir?"

"Stay?"

She glanced upward, toward the second story. "I couldn't go on sleeping in that grand room at the top of the stairs. Not if I'm to be a maid. That wouldn't be proper."

He rubbed his jaw, considering. She was right. It wouldn't be proper.

Mrs. Adler had her own quarters at the back of the house. Chuck, the cook, slept in a small room attached to the bunkhouse. As for the guest cottage, it had become Roger's art studio last summer. Even now, half-finished canvases and supplies filled the two rooms.

That would have to change. Tomorrow.

That night, Keely sat on the edge of the grand bed in the second-floor bedroom, mulling over all that had transpired in a single day. When she'd departed Pocatello in the hired rig, she'd expected to find Roger Bernhardt at the end of the road. Expected him to greet her with kindness. To rescue her, perhaps, like a prince in one of the old Brothers Grimm tales.

But would he have wanted to rescue her? Especially if he knew how she'd paid for her passage to America?

She gave her head a sharp shake. She couldn't think about that. What was done was done. Her mam used to tell her, "You can't change the past, Keely, but you can choose how to live so your future looks different." Dwelling on mistakes helped nothing.

Besides, she'd done what she had to do to get away. There had been no other choice. What would've happened to her if she'd stayed at the manor with Mr. Brown still there?

No, that was unthinkable.

She squeezed her eyes shut, willing away the memory of her last day at Hooke Manor.

A door closed somewhere in the house, the sound faint but distinct, and she startled. It reminded her that she wasn't alone. Not truly. And as if summoned by the thought, an image of William Overstreet rose in her mind, pushing aside all others.

He had been her unexpected rescuer, though he bore no resemblance to any prince or knight from a fairy tale. She recalled how he'd looked when he'd entered the parlor earlier—boots crusted with dried mud, hair tousled, jaw dark with stubble. He could've turned her away. A lesser man might have done so without a second thought.

In a fairy tale, a villain would have thrown her to the wolves. But William had welcomed her. Invited her to dine at his table. Treated her, if only for a time, as an equal.

"And now I'm to work for him."

To work for him at Eden's Gate as a housemaid. The very lie she'd told the officials at Ellis Island had somehow come true.

She rose from the bed and slowly undressed, exchanging her travel-worn blouse and skirt for a clean nightgown. Shortly after, she extinguished the bedside table lamp, casting the room into darkness.

Kneeling beside the bed, she clasped her hands together, just as her mam had taught her when she was still a little girl with skinned knees and tangled curls.

"God," she whispered, "please forgive me for taking her ladyship's things. Forgive me for the lies I told to get all the way to this place. I could not have done it any other way. I'm sure of it. Even so, I know in Your eyes 'twas wrong." Her throat tightened. "Tell Mam I'm sorry. Amen."

She rose, climbed into the bed, and tucked herself beneath the heavy covers. The warmth of the thick blanket wrapped around her, holding the chill at bay. She stared into the darkness for a while longer, listening to the silence of the house and the quiet howl of wind outside the window.

Despite everything, her heart found a thread of peace.

She had made it to Idaho. And by God's grace, perhaps she had found a new beginning as well.

Chapter Three

The next morning, Keely stood erect and silent in front of Mrs. Adler while the older woman eyed her from head to toe.

"Do you own another skirt?" the housekeeper asked at last.

"One, ma'am. But this is the better of the two. Same for me blouse."

Mrs. Adler sighed. "Well, I suppose it doesn't matter. Mr. William has few visitors these days. Can you sew?"

"Yes, ma'am. I'm good with a needle and thread."

"Then I'll see that you get some fabric. Even if you don't stay on at Eden's Gate, you'll need a new dress or two for future employment."

Keely nodded, well aware of the disapproval in the woman's tone—disapproval of giving her fabric, of bringing a new maid into the house, of Keely Boyle herself.

"Our first order of business is clearing out the

cottage," Mrs. Adler said crisply. "It seems that's where Mr. William intends for you to sleep from now on."

The cottage? Keely didn't dare ask where it was.

"It's chock-full of canvases and who knows what else. What Mr. William expects us to do with it all, I don't have a clue. Back into the shed, I suppose." Mrs. Adler grabbed a bibbed apron off a hook on the kitchen wall. "Put this on and come with me. We may as well get started."

Keely followed quickly, fumbling to tie the apron strings into a bow behind her as she walked. Fortunately, they didn't have far to go. The cottage stood just across the barnyard—a single-story stone building, fashioned from the same sturdy rock as the big house.

"No one's stayed in here since before Mr. Bernhardt painted that splendid picture of a buffalo," Mrs. Adler remarked. "They only used it for guests until then."

She pushed open the door, and as it swung inward, a warm, nutty scent met them. Linseed oil, old and mellow. Beneath it came the sharper tang of aged turpentine. Windows covered on the inside cast the room in shadows. Mrs. Adler moved to open the shutters, her motions brisk.

Following close behind, Keely stepped inside.

Light spilled gradually across the space, revealing a world draped in linen dust cloths. An easel stood like a forgotten sentry in the corner. Crates leaned against the far wall, several with their lids ajar, showing the edges of framed canvases.

Mrs. Adler set down a basket of cleaning supplies.

"With a little airing and elbow grease, it won't smell this bad for long."

Keely didn't mind the smell. It reminded her of Roger. He'd almost always painted during his visits to Hooke Manor, and these very scents—linseed and turpentine—had clung to his clothes, just as paint lingered beneath his fingernails.

A sharp rap sounded on the doorjamb behind her. She spun around.

William Overstreet stood framed in the doorway, several other men behind him. "We've come to move the crates before we head out."

"Thank goodness." Mrs. Adler stepped forward. "I didn't know how we'd clean with all of that in the way." She caught Keely's arm and guided her aside, making room for the men to enter, each of them giving Keely a curious stare as they passed through the doorway. But they soon focused their attention on their work and began hauling crates from the room.

Only then did Keely notice the doorway leading to a second room. A small bedroom—modest but complete—with a bed, a wingback chair, a wardrobe and bureau, and a writing desk tucked beneath the window.

This was to be where she stayed while working as a maid? Her chest tightened. No wonder Mrs. Adler's face had been so pinched with disapproval.

The housekeeper began issuing orders as soon as the men had removed the last crate. Keely's first task was to roll up the rugs and take them outside to beat the dust from them, while Mrs. Adler swept and mopped the floors. By the time Keely returned, shivering from the brisk morning air, a fire crackled in the wood stove, chasing the chill from the cottage.

"Help me with the furniture, please," Mrs. Adler said.

They moved the table and two ladder-back chairs away from the walls, followed by the sofa and matching stuffed chair. Then they dusted shelves, wiped down books, and polished the window glass until the little parlor gleamed.

At last, Mrs. Adler straightened and gave a brisk nod. "I'll leave you to clean the bedroom and the water closet. I've things to see to in the house."

"There's a water closet?"

The housekeeper gave her a sharp look. "Girl, didn't you notice the other door in the bedroom? You'll not last long in these parts if you don't pay attention to your surroundings. Danger can lurk anywhere. You hear me?"

"Yes, ma'am."

Mrs. Adler paused by the door. "Now, don't dawdle. Mr. Kincaid will have lunch ready in half an hour."

Keely had already been told that, while William and the cowboys called the ranch cook Chuck, she was to address him by his proper name—Mr. Kincaid. That was easy enough to remember. Showing respect to one's betters was one of the first lessons learned in service. And on this ranch, everyone was her better. She knew it well.

"Yes, ma'am," she replied again.

When the door closed behind Mrs. Adler, Keely stepped into the bedroom and crossed to the narrow second door. She opened it and stared in wonder.

There was, indeed, a water closet. A porcelain bowl

with a high-mounted tank and chain for flushing, and a lavatory sink with a hand pump similar to the one she'd seen in the kitchen.

Indoor plumbing.

It was rare enough anywhere. To find it here, in a modest guest cottage on a ranch in Idaho, felt nothing short of miraculous.

A wave of shame rose within her. She didn't deserve this. Not a job. Not a cottage. Not this kindness.

And certainly not forgiveness.

William bumped the brim of his hat with his knuckles, pushing it off his forehead as he peered up at the sky. Clouds were gathering in the west.

"Might bring rain," Jake Foster said beside him.

"Might," William replied, "but I doubt it."

"Headed back to the house?"

He nodded. "Sent word for Roger and Victoria to come for lunch. Hopefully, they could get away."

"Mrs. Bernhardt done teaching school?"

"Yeah. The board let her keep the post after the wedding, but once they found out she was expecting a baby, they got serious about finding someone else. New teacher was supposed to start this week."

"Shame. She seemed to enjoy it."

"She did. But she'll have plenty to keep her busy once the baby arrives toward the end of summer." William nudged Skunk, his five-year-old stallion, with his heels and rode off toward the barn.

There was genuine warmth in the sun on the first day of April. Almost enough to make him shrug off his jacket. Almost, but not quite. Spring had always been his favorite season. Colts and calves filled the paddocks. Puppies and kittens usually turned up in the barn or beneath the porch. Pale green leaves unfurled on trees that had stood bare for months.

Sensing the barn ahead, Skunk broke from a canter into a gallop, and William didn't rein him in. It felt good to give the stallion his head. He leaned forward, letting the wind sting his cheeks as he recalled the frosty February morning when Skunk was born—his coat black as night with a narrow white stripe down the center of his rump, vanishing into his tail.

"Boss, you raising skunks now?" Rocky Turner had joked that morning.

The unfortunate name had stuck. But in the years since, the stallion had become William's favorite ranch horse. Smart, quick, and smooth as silk under rein. And despite remaining a stud, Skunk had an easy-going nature that suited William well.

He wondered if his new housemaid had the same. That wild red hair made him doubt it. But then, it wasn't really his concern. More Mrs. Adler's than his own, even though he'd been the one to offer the girl a job.

He set the thought aside and drew back on the reins, slowing Skunk to a gentle lope as the ranch buildings came into view. A few minutes later, he spotted the Bernhardt buggy already in the barnyard. Roger was just helping Victoria down from the seat.

"Hello!" William called, drawing their attention. He reined in nearby and dropped down from the saddle. "Glad you could make it on such short notice."

Roger grinned. "I daresay the summons intrigued us."

"Did it sound like a summons? Didn't mean for it to. However, we had an unexpected visitor yesterday, and I figured you'd want to know."

Roger's brow furrowed. "A visitor?"

"Come inside, and I'll explain."

Tom Flores stepped out of the barn and, with no need of direction, crossed to take Skunk's reins. William acknowledged him with a nod, then turned toward the house. Roger offered Victoria his arm, and the three of them made their way across the yard to the porch and front door.

Once inside, they settled into the front parlor— Roger on the settee beside his wife, William in the nearby chair.

"So . . ." Roger said, one brow lifted. "Tell us about this unexpected visitor. And why we should care."

"Because she came to see you," William replied.

"She?" Roger and Victoria said in unison.

William suddenly wondered if he'd mishandled the situation. It was one thing to spring the news of Keely's arrival at the ranch on Roger. However it wasn't fair for him to do it to Victoria. But what could he do about it? How could he get Roger off by himself now that he'd begun?

"Who is it?" Roger asked, frowning.

Before William could answer, Mrs. Adler appeared in the dining room doorway, a tea tray balanced in her hands. And right behind her stood Keely Boyle.

At the sight of Roger, Keely's eyes went wide. All the color drained from her face. "Mr. Bernhardt, sir," she whispered—before crumpling to the floor in a dead faint.

William was on his feet in an instant. He rushed to her side and knelt. "Mrs. Adler, get me a damp cloth. Please."

"At once, Mr. William." She bustled off to the kitchen.

Keely's eyelids fluttered.

"Miss Boyle?" he said gently.

She blinked. Once. Twice. Then again.

"That's better." He offered a small smile. "Can you see me?"

"Yes, sir." Her voice was soft, faraway.

"Good."

Mrs. Adler returned and handed him the damp cloth. He placed it on Keely's forehead.

"Just lie still a moment," he said when she tried to lift her head.

"I'll be askin' what happened?"

Roger stepped forward. "I daresay you fainted, Keely Boyle."

"Don't be daft," she muttered. After a moment, seeming to realize who'd spoken to her, she turned her head toward Roger. Then, spurred into action, she scrambled to her feet, the damp cloth falling, forgotten, to the floor. "Sure and that's never happened to me before." Her cheeks flamed with color.

Roger chuckled. "Well, this is a surprise for me as well. To see you anywhere other than Hooke Manor. Perhaps I'm the one who should have fainted."

"Yes, sir. I mean, no, sir." Her fingers brushed her apron, though the gesture seemed more about calming nerves than dusting off dirt. "'Tis only a surprise to me too. To be here."

Roger looked at William. "Mr. Overstreet hasn't yet had the chance to explain how that came to be."

"Then we'd best take care of that." He motioned them all back toward the parlor.

Chapter Four

How could she tell any of them the truth?

Keely sank into the nearest chair and clenched her hands in her lap, waiting for the questions she knew must come. Last night, she'd asked God to forgive her for the lies she'd told and the money and possessions she'd stolen. She feared she'd be begging for that forgiveness all over again before the day was done. Especially now, with Roger Bernhardt seated on the settee beside his wife.

A little piece of her heart seemed to break all over again as she looked at them. She'd once imagined Roger putting his arm around *her* shoulders, the way he did now with Victoria. She'd wanted him to love her the way she thought she'd loved him.

Silly girl.

Did I ever love him?

The answer came swiftly.

No.

She remembered how it had been between her mam

and da—the gentle touches, the whispered words, the quiet laughter between them. There had been tenderness. Understanding. Genuine affection.

It had never been that way with her and Roger. She'd admired him from afar, perhaps even been infatuated. But love? No. Just a young girl's longing, a romantic notion she'd mistaken for something deeper. She'd realized the truth even before fleeing Hooke Manor to escape Mr. Brown's threats.

She closed her eyes, trying to push back the wave of fear rising in her throat. Fear . . . and shame. Shame . . . and dread.

"Perhaps I should begin," Roger said after a lengthy silence. "I became acquainted with Miss Boyle at Hooke Manor where she was employed. As I recall, she liked to watch me paint when I came for a visit, and we would exchange a few words now and then. Isn't that right, Keely?"

"Yes, sir."

"But whatever caused you to uproot yourself and come to America? I don't remember you ever saying you wished to do such a thing."

She didn't realize she was crying until she heard Victoria say, "Gentlemen, I believe you should leave us alone for a while."

"Victoria—" Roger began.

"Please, darling."

Keely sniffed and wiped her eyes with the corner of her apron. When she looked up again, the men were gone. She and Victoria were alone in the parlor.

"May I call you Keely?"

She nodded.

"You must call me Victoria."

"I'm thinking that wouldn't be right."

"Of course it is."

Keely shook her head, fresh tears brimming.

"I'm Roger's wife." Victoria moved closer on the settee and offered a handkerchief.

Keely accepted it with a whispered, "Thank you," dabbing at her cheeks.

"He said he knew you in England."

"Yes, ma'am."

"Would you tell me more?"

Keely swallowed the lump in her throat. "I was a housemaid at Hooke Manor. Mr. Bernhardt is a friend of his lordship. The earl's son. Well, his lordship is the earl now, but he wasn't yet when Mr. Bernhardt came to America."

"And Roger was kind to you, wasn't he?"

She nodded. "Always kind. Not just to me. To everyone. Good and truly, he was."

"I know. He showed me many kindnesses when we first met." Victoria smiled softly, her expression tinged with remembrance. "He's that sort of man."

"Yes, ma'am." Keely wiped her eyes again.

Victoria drew a deep breath. "Will you tell me *why* you came to America, Keely?"

The answer came more easily than she expected. "Because I was afraid to stay at the manor any longer."

And once she'd spoken that one truth, the rest came pouring out. Mr. Brown's assault and her narrow escape. Her certainty that he would try again if given the chance.

The letter from Roger, sent to Lord and Lady Hooke, full of praise for America and all the freedom it offered. The painting he'd included, showing the mountain range visible from this very house. Even the lies she'd told to pass the inspections at Ellis Island.

The only truth she held back was how she'd paid for her passage—with money and jewelry stolen from her ladyship, the Countess of Hooke. She couldn't bear for William or Roger or even Victoria to know that. Not when the person she'd stolen from was the sister of the man who had just given her employment.

When her words finally ran dry, Keely fell silent, eyes downcast. The very room seemed to hold its breath.

At last, Victoria spoke. "I'll ask only one thing. Why didn't you tell your mistress what Mr. Brown tried to do to you? Why didn't you tell anyone at Hooke Manor?"

"No one would've believed me. Lord Brandish is held in high regard. That means his man—Mr. Brown—is respected below stairs. I'm only a housemaid. An Irish housemaid. My word would never stand against his. And even if they had believed me, they'd say it was me own fault. That I brought it on meself. Even if I wasn't sacked, no one would have looked at me the same ever again."

"I see." Victoria's voice was quiet. She let out a long breath. "I'm sorry you believe that to be true. I hope you're wrong."

Keely looked up, her vision blurred by fresh tears.

Victoria reached out and patted her clenched hands. "But I believe you. You can trust me as you trusted Roger. Do you believe me?"

Keely sniffed as she nodded.

"Good. Now I'm going to have a word with my husband and William. You needn't worry. Just wait here. I won't be long." With that, she stood and slipped from the parlor. Moments later, a door closed somewhere down the hall, followed by the hum of muffled voices.

Heat rushed to Keely's cheeks as she imagined Victoria sharing everything she'd just confessed with Roger and William Overstreet. Would they send her away now? Now that they knew she was a liar? Worse, would they believe she was at fault for what Mr. Brown had tried to do?

The sound of footsteps pulled her to her feet just as Victoria returned, with Roger and William behind her. Keely looked from one face to the next, searching for her fate in their expressions.

William lingered in the hallway while Victoria and Roger entered the parlor. He watched as the couple settled on the settee, Victoria between her husband and Keely. Victoria reached for the other woman's hand and spoke gently, her voice just loud enough to carry into the hallway.

"You won't be sent away, Keely. You're safe here."

William turned at those words and walked back to his study, closing the door softly behind him.

A few minutes earlier, Roger had said, "If you don't want her working here as a maid, I'll understand. She came here because she knew me, and I feel responsible for her."

It was true. William's offer of employment had been made on impulse—quick, unexamined, born from the moment. He hadn't thought it through. Hadn't expected it to last long. But now, knowing the full story, he couldn't send Keely Boyle away.

Not when her story sounded all too familiar.

Her name was Pearl.

She'd worked as a housemaid in the Manhattan mansion of Phillip Morgan, a wealthy banker and close friend of William's father, David Overstreet. William had been back from England nearly a year by then, still trying to find his place in the shipping business under his father's stern instruction.

That night, there'd been a ball at the Morgan home. The guests weren't the cream of New York society. Not a single name among them would have been listed among Ward McAllister's Four Hundred. The scent of new money had clung too heavily to those in the ballroom for that.

As the hour neared midnight, William had slipped away from the crowd, tired of empty conversation with ambitious young women who seemed more inter-ested in his family name than in him. He wanted silence. Space. Something resembling the open air and quiet of the Overstreet ranch in Idaho. What he wouldn't have given in that moment for a saddle beneath him, a galloping horse, and the scent of sage on the wind.

He was wandering down a darkened hallway when

he heard it—muffled sobbing. At first, he thought he'd imagined it. But then he heard it again.

He followed the sound and found a girl sitting on the landing of the back stairway. Her dress was torn, her hair disheveled, her maid's cap missing. She scrambled backward at the sight of him, eyes wide with terror.

He knew, even before she spoke, what had happened.

Pearl had been assaulted—raped—by a guest at the party. A man of means who had taken what he wanted, believing himself entitled. The pain in her voice, the shame in her eyes. William never doubted her. He had tried to help her, tried to report what she told him.

But no one had listened.

He'd been too young, too powerless, too easily dismissed. There was no investigation. No arrest. No justice. And when he heard, weeks later, that Pearl had taken her own life, something inside him had broken.

It remained broken even now.

He had failed Pearl.

But he would not fail Keely Boyle.

That was why he'd offered her a place at Eden's Gate, even knowing full well that Mrs. Adler had no use for another servant. That was why, when he'd seen the fear in Keely's eyes, he'd known instinctively that she must be protected.

She could stay. As long as she needed. As long as she wanted.

Drawing a steady breath, William stood and left the study a second time.

The parlor was quiet when he entered, save for Keely's soft sniffles. She sat with her shoulders slightly hunched, dabbing at her eyes with a handkerchief, gaze fixed on her lap.

A slow heat built in William's chest as he imagined a man laying unwanted hands on her. It stirred something fierce and protective deep within him.

Roger looked up. "Keely tells us the cottage is to be hers."

William gave a single nod.

"I take it I need to borrow a wagon," Roger continued, "so I can move the rest of my paintings into town."

"That'd be best. The shed's only a temporary fix. Can't promise they'll be safe from weather or critters out there. If you want, we can load them before you leave today. One of the boys can drive the wagon into Gibeon for you."

Roger turned to Victoria, grinning. "Perfect timing, actually. Yesterday we rented the old Mason building. We're going to use it as a studio and gallery. I daresay I can hang the ones I like best."

William offered a smile but said nothing. He couldn't help marveling at the change in his friend.

Roger Bernhardt, who once claimed he had no intention of settling anywhere, was now a man deeply rooted. He had a wife. A child on the way. A house in town. A future that reached beyond the next painting or passing season. He had embraced responsibility and found happiness in it.

William admired that. He was even glad of it.

But if he was honest with himself, a whisper of envy stirred in his chest. Envy for the new life he was making *with* someone. The steadiness of it. The peace.

Before he could dwell on it further, Mrs. Adler's voice rang out from the dining room doorway. "Lunch is ready, Mr. William."

Pushing aside thoughts better left unspoken, William straightened and motioned for his guests to follow him.

"Come on," he said. "Let's eat."

Chapter Five

Three days later, Keely sat in the surrey's backseat beside Mrs. Adler as the horse trotted toward town. William sat alone on the front bench, the leather reins threaded through his gloved fingers. A handful of cowboys followed on horseback, their conversation indistinct beneath the rhythm of hooves on packed earth.

Keely wished she'd been allowed to stay behind at the ranch. Though she'd asked God for forgiveness—for the lies, for the theft—she wasn't convinced He'd granted it. Truth be told, she wasn't even sure He heard her anymore.

Sure and He stopped listening to me a long time ago.

Not that she blamed Him. She hadn't lived the way her mam had raised her. Why would the Almighty want her in church, sitting on a pew, pretending to be a good Christian? Wasn't that just another lie?

She'd told enough of those already.

She turned her gaze to the landscape rolling past—

golden grass and early spring blossoms leading to mountains rising blue and noble in the distance—but it was her mam's face she saw in her mind. Despite the poverty that had dogged them after Da passed, Mam had trusted God. She'd prayed daily, praised Him in song, even on days when there was no bread in the house and no firewood to burn. Her faith had been unshakable.

Keely's was barely there by comparison. She wanted to be a good Christian but was fairly certain the Lord lost track of her the day she emigrated to England. She had become invisible. Forgotten. Even by the God of heaven.

But, like it or not, she was on her way to church even though she didn't quite measure up. Because it was expected. Because William Overstreet and his household were going. Because she didn't want to cause offense. So she would smile. Say the right things. Sit quietly and look pleasant. She would pretend innocence when she was anything but.

Her chest tightened, and she closed her eyes, trying to shut out the shame pressing in. What an ungrateful wretch she was. William had given her employment and the loveliest place she'd ever lived. Mrs. Adler, for all her sternness, had a tender heart. Roger and Victoria Bernhardt had welcomed her into their lives, promising she could come to them with any problem. They'd shown her nothing but kindness, all of them, despite knowing she'd lied to get through immigration and find her way to Idaho.

But would they be so forgiving if they knew she was a thief as well? And not just once. The money and jewelry taken from the countess hadn't been the first time she'd helped herself to what wasn't hers.

Oh, Mam . . . You would be so ashamed of me.

"There's Gibeon up ahead," William called over his shoulder, his voice raised above the clatter of wheels and the steady beat of hooves.

Keely opened her eyes and leaned slightly to the side for a better view. The church came into sight first— white-painted, modest, and unmistakable with its steeple. Beyond it stretched the little town: a wide street flanked by low buildings, brown and dusty, leafless trees planted near storefronts and porches. It wasn't much to look at.

Odd, she thought. A town, just . . . plopped down in the middle of nowhere.

Then again, wasn't that how every town in America had begun? Even great cities like New York had started small. Empty land, a few brave settlers, and then the slow building of something lasting.

As the surrey approached the church, Keely saw others walking in that direction. Wagons and riders came from all sides. Voices called out greetings. Laughter rang through the crisp morning air. Small groups gathered on the steps and along the street, talking, visiting.

Nerves twisted in Keely's stomach. She had spent so many years feeling invisible, unnoticed. She'd hated it. But just now, she would give anything not to be seen.

William reined in the horse and brought the surrey to a halt. After tying the animal to a hitching post, he returned to help Mrs. Adler alight. Keely accepted his hand next, grateful for the steadiness it offered as she touched ground.

Once on her feet, she moved closer to the house-keeper, wishing again she had stayed behind.

"No call to be nervous," Mrs. Adler said quietly. "These are good people."

Before Keely could answer, she spotted Roger Bernhardt walking toward them, his hand resting gently on Victoria's arm. The couple looked every bit the picture of happiness. Smiling. At ease.

How had she ever imagined that a man like Roger might fall in love with someone like her?

Foolish girl.

She looked at William then—at the man who had given her this second chance—and a chill swept down her spine. She'd stolen from his sister to get here. What would he do if he found out? Would he cast her out? Would he take back everything he'd offered?

Guilt warred with the hard truth of her reality.

Yes, Jocelyn Whitcombe, Countess of Hooke, was wealthy beyond anything Keely could imagine. The money she'd taken was a drop in the bucket to her ladyship. A handful of banknotes, a bracelet Jocelyn rarely wore, a beautiful necklace, a pair of earrings, a simple brooch. To someone like the countess, it all meant nothing.

But to Keely? It had meant salvation.

Even so, the weight of what she'd done pressed down like a boulder. In her mind, she heard Mam's gentle voice, full of sorrow. *Aye, me darlin' girl. It is terrible what you've done. Sure and you know 'tis true.*

"Good morning, Keely," Roger said as they reached her.

"Mornin', Mr. Bernhardt."

Victoria stepped forward and touched Keely's arm. "We're glad you're here. Come with me, and I'll introduce you to a few people."

"That isn't necessary," Keely said quickly.

"Of course it is." Victoria's tone left no room for argument. She slipped her arm through Keely's and smiled. "Come along. These people are your neighbors now. And soon enough, they'll be your friends. Just as they've become friends of mine."

With that, Victoria gently guided her away from the others.

William and Roger stood side by side, watching as Victoria led Keely toward a small cluster of women near the chapel entrance. Mrs. Adler followed a few steps behind them, her posture stiff, her gaze watchful—like a mother hen guarding her chicks.

"How is she doing?" Roger asked.

"Keely?" William kept his eyes on the group ahead. "Well enough, I think. She seems to be a good worker. No complaints from Mrs. Adler, at any rate." He gave a small shrug. "I see little of her, to be honest. I'm out on the range most days, and she takes her meals in the kitchen with Mrs. Adler and Chuck."

He didn't add that just the night before, he'd come within a breath of carrying his dinner plate into the kitchen to join them. He'd missed the sound of voices at his table. Once, he'd relished the peace and quiet of solitary meals. Now, they left him feeling more alone than rested.

Of course, if he had joined them, Mrs. Adler might have fainted right there on the spot, much like Keely had done a few days ago.

Keely.

His gaze found her again. Victoria had brought her to the edge of the group now, making introductions to Reverend Blankenship. Keely's cheeks were flushed, and she kept her eyes lowered, refusing to meet the pastor's gaze. Even from across the churchyard, William sensed her discomfort.

"She's nervous," he said.

Roger followed his gaze. "Can't say I blame her. She's been through more than most, and now she's starting over in a new world." He clapped a hand on William's shoulder. "Come on. We'd best go in."

Gibeon Chapel had been built by its congregation in 1885, better than fifteen years after the town was founded. From the outside, it resembled countless churches scattered across the West—simple whitewashed siding, narrow windows set in even rows, and a steeple that reached toward heaven. Nothing fancy. Just the work of calloused hands and willing hearts.

Back then, the congregation had been served by a circuit rider. There'd been several of those over the years, both before and after the church building was erected. Pastor Robinson for a time. Reverend Jones for a couple of years. Pastor Gill for a shorter spell. One or two others after him. The hope had been that a church building would eventually bring them a permanent pastor, and that hope was fulfilled with the appointment of Truman Blankenship, a young man—barely twenty at the time— with quite an old soul.

As William stepped into the sanctuary behind Roger, he looked around as though seeing the place for the first time. As if trying to see it anew through Keely's eyes.

Pale morning sunlight filtered through the windows, casting soft, golden rectangles across the wide-planked floor. The pews, worn smooth by worshippers, stood in two straight rows, divided by a center aisle. At the front of the room, a raised platform held a sturdy pulpit, hand-carved long ago by one of the congregation's founding members. Behind it, a plain wooden cross stood quietly against the wall—no ornamentation, no embellishment. Just the symbol of their faith.

To the right of the platform sat an upright piano, its dark wood dulled with age, but the keys still bright and ready to lead hearts in praise.

There was nothing grand about the chapel, but it carried a warmth William felt deep in his chest. The space did not aim to impress. It was meant to welcome. A place where weary souls could come and remember that they were not alone.

He slid into his usual pew, Roger and Victoria beside him. As he settled, William glanced over his shoulder. Keely had found a place in the row just behind, seated between Mrs. Adler and Jake Foster. The color had drained from her face, and she pressed her lips into a thin line. No smile. No ease in her posture. A fish out of water, no doubt.

William turned back around, his thoughts quieting as the familiar strains of the piano filled the room. Bertha Hathaway's hands moved deftly over the keys, and a moment later Reverend Truman Blankenship stepped onto the platform.

"Please rise and turn in your hymnals to number two hundred," Truman said, his voice rich and calm. "'All Hail the Power of Jesus' Name.'"

William didn't reach for a hymnal. He didn't need to. The words had lived in his heart for years. He stood, lifted his voice, and sang. "All hail the power of Jesus' Name! / Let angels prostrate fall, / Bring forth the royal diadem, / And crown Him Lord of all; / Bring forth the royal diadem, / And crown Him Lord of all."

As the voices around him rose in harmony, something shifted in his chest. The loneliness that had been quietly gnawing at him these past weeks melted away, like frost touched by sun. God had been good to him. God was always good to him and would be good to him tomorrow. Steadily, faithfully, always. He knew that. He believed it.

The Lord is my shepherd; I shall not want. The words of Psalm 23 came to him unbidden, and he let them nestle in his soul.

It was better—wiser—to remember what he had rather than long for what he didn't. To be content in the life God had given him. Purpose existed in this place, in his work, and in the people he was responsible for.

Yes, better to lift his voice in praise than waste another moment on regrets.

Chapter Six

The study door creaked softly as Keely eased it open. She'd been on the Overstreet ranch a full week now, first sleeping in the upstairs bedchamber, now in the guest cottage. She'd cleaned most of the rooms in the big house, dusted bookshelves, washed windows, mopped the kitchen floor more than once.

But this was the first time she'd stepped inside what she silently called the master's domain.

She hesitated on the threshold, feather duster in hand, the stillness of the room pressing in around her. It felt different here. More private. As if she'd crossed into a place not meant for servants.

A massive desk dominated the space, worn smooth with use. Daylight spilled through the west-facing window, pooling on the polished wood floor in a golden hush. Books and ledgers lined shelves along two walls, their spines tidy, dustless. The air held a faint, lingering scent of pipe tobacco, mixed with the sharper tang of oiled leather from the armchair near the hearth.

She stepped inside and closed the door behind her.

Starting at the bookshelf, she swept the feather duster lightly over the rows of bindings, careful not to disturb the arrangement. From there, she moved to the fireplace mantel. A few keepsakes stood in a neat row: a silver watch fob, a hand-carved wooden horse no larger than her thumb, and a smooth, flat stone the color of river clay—the kind boys liked to skim across ponds or streams.

Her fingers hovered above the stone, then gently picked it up. Warmed by the afternoon sun, it rested in her palm as if it had always belonged there.

Not just any stone, she thought. Not to the man who had placed it here. Back in Ireland, she'd seen village men keep small tokens like this—reminders of a journey, a place, a loss. Markers of a memory that mattered.

Had William Overstreet found this stone as a boy? Carried it with him through some sorrow or hardship? Was it a piece of home, a piece of heart?

Her chest tightened. A familiar ache stirred, one she'd hoped to leave behind in England. That subtle pull toward small, pocketable things. The hunger to take something and keep it close. Something that wasn't hers.

She had told herself in the past that she only ever took what she needed. Nothing more. But the memory of her final theft, those coins and banknotes from her mistress's bureau, rose unbidden. The money and the jewels had been enough to buy her passage across both ocean and continent, yes. But the cost had been far greater than money.

This wasn't money. Just a stone. Yet the old hunger whispered. So did the old fear, a fear that someday she would be left with nothing again. As she'd been after her da died. As she'd felt the day Mr. Brown tried to take more than her dignity.

She glanced toward the door. The house was still. No one else was about. Curling her fingers around the stone, she slipped it into the pocket of her apron. It was no heavier than a breath, yet somehow it seemed to weigh her down, as if it carried the burden of every wrong she'd ever tried to forget.

Her hand lingered on the mantel one last time before she turned back to her work. Her motions were brisk now, almost sharp, as if speed could scrub away guilt.

Then came a faint creak.

She froze, the duster trembling in her grip. Turning slowly, she found William standing in the doorway.

"Miss Boyle." His voice was warm enough, but her name landed like a bell rung too loud in a silent room.

She dipped her head quickly, praying her cheeks wouldn't betray her. "Sir."

He stepped into the room and crossed to the desk, setting his hat on the corner. His gaze swept the space, lingering a fraction too long on the mantel. Her fingers clenched around the duster's handle.

"You've been here a week now," he said at last, his tone casual. "I've been meaning to ask how you're settling in. Everything to your satisfaction?"

Her heart still pounded. "Yes, sir. 'Tis . . . a fine place." She shifted her weight from one foot to the other, desperate to finish her dusting and be gone.

He leaned a hip against the desk, arms folded loosely. "And the cottage? You've all you need there?"

"Aye. 'Tis more than I could ever hope for, to be sure."

She risked a glance upward. His hazel eyes met hers—not unkind, but direct in a way that made her wish for something to do with her hands.

"Mrs. Adler says you've taken to the work well."

"That's kind of her."

His gaze flicked toward the mantel again. Quick, almost casual. But not quick enough. Keely noticed. And in that instant, she was certain he knew. Knew something was missing. Knew it was her. Knew everything.

She fought to keep her breath steady.

He nodded slowly. "If you find you lack anything, you've only to speak up."

She swallowed. "I will, sir."

Silence stretched between them, filled only by the ticking of the clock. He seemed in no hurry. But every beat of her heart thudded with urgency.

"If that's all," she said, her voice coming faster than she intended, "I should be about the rest of the rooms."

One corner of his mouth lifted, as if he heard her unspoken panic. "Of course. I'll not keep you."

She brushed past him with care, avoiding even the slightest contact with his sleeve, and slipped out the door. Not until she'd reached the halfway point of the hallway did she let herself breathe.

She pressed a hand to her apron pocket, fingers closing over the stone.

It was still there.

But instead of comfort, the knowledge of it filled her with a fresh wave of shame.

William stared at the closed door for a long moment, as if willing it to reveal what lay on the other side. Something about the way Keely had slipped out—too quickly, too carefully—niggled at the back of his mind. She'd avoided touching him, avoided looking at him straight on. And while he couldn't put his finger on why, the moment felt . . . off.

He exhaled slowly and turned toward the desk. The late-afternoon sun slanted through the west-facing window, casting long golden bars across the floorboards and stretching toward the mantel. His gaze drifted there, and a frown tugged at his brow.

Something wasn't right.

He crossed the room, eyes narrowing as he took in the familiar arrangement. The silver watch fob still sat in its place. So did the small carved horse. But the flat stone, the one that had rested between them, was gone.

He stood motionless. It was just a stone. Worthless to anyone else. But the space where it used to sit seemed to press painfully on his heart.

Memory stirred, vivid and immediate. A summer afternoon high in the mountain forest. The bright gleam of sunlight on water. His mother's laughter echoing off the trees. He'd been twelve years old—barefoot, sunbrowned, with scabbed knees from rough play—skipping rocks across the icy-clear swimming hole near their campsite. The stone he'd held was river-clay brown with a streak of pale orange running across it. It had skipped six times. His personal record. The "lucky one," he'd called it before diving in to retrieve it from the bottom of the pond. For reasons he never quite understood, he'd kept it all these years.

When he was sent to England, the stone had crossed the Atlantic with him. It had sat in his pocket through the loneliest years of his schooling, a link to home when everything around him felt foreign. He'd held it the day the letter came, telling him his mother had died. And it had come back with him again, first to New York, and then to the one place that had ever truly felt like his—this ranch. His mother's ranch.

And now the stone was gone.

His jaw clenched.

The house was quiet—Mrs. Adler and Chuck would be in the kitchen, the hands outside tending to the usual end-of-day chores. That left only Keely. She'd been dusting the mantel not ten minutes ago. He remembered how her eyes had darted to his, then quickly away, as though afraid of what he might read there.

He rubbed the back of his neck, then crouched beside the hearth and scanned the rug, the floorboards. Nothing. The mantel was deep. A careless knock wouldn't have sent the stone far. But it was nowhere in sight.

He stood again, slower this time.

He wasn't about to accuse her. Not over something so small. And yet . . . it wasn't small. Not to him.

There was no good reason for Keely—or anyone—to take the stone. Maybe she'd thought it had been misplaced, a piece of debris to throw back outside or in the rubbish bin. Or maybe it had simply been knocked off the mantel while she dusted, and someone would find it in the coming days, wedged beneath a baseboard.

Surely, he told himself, it will turn up.

He rested his hands on the edge of the mantel and stared at the space where the stone had once sat, trying not to think about what it might mean to him if no one ever found it.

A sharp knock at the door snapped him out of his thoughts.

"Come in," he called, stepping back.

Jake Foster entered, hat in hand, lines etched deep into his weathered face from decades beneath the Idaho sun. "Sorry to bother you, boss. Figured you'd want to know. We found a dead cow and her calf along the southern fence line."

William straightened, the personal loss shoved aside as duty took over. "When?"

"'Bout an hour ago. I was riding fence with Logan. At first, we thought maybe they'd just gone down in a bad spot, but . . ." Jake shook his head. "Coyotes had already been at 'em by the time we got there. Hard to say what happened beforehand."

William's mouth tightened. "Think it could've been wolves? Or another grizzly?"

"Not a grizzly. No claw marks or tearing like from a bear. Maybe wolves instead of coyotes. We've seen signs up in the foothills this winter, but not much since the thaw. No fresh tracks around the bodies, though. Ground's too dry."

He nodded grimly. "What about sickness?"

Jake shrugged. "Doesn't look like it. The herd in that section's been strong. No signs of illness last I checked, and the cow had good weight on her for coming out of winter."

William rubbed the back of his neck again, the muscles tight. "Could she have stepped in a gopher hole? Broken a leg? That'd leave her and the calf vulnerable to coyotes."

"Thought of that. But no broken bones I could find. And the calf . . . Well, she was torn up too bad to say for sure." Jake hesitated, then added, "It's strange, boss. I can't put my finger on it, but it don't feel right. Like there's more to it than a couple of unlucky animals."

William's expression darkened. "We'll keep a close watch on the herd. Anything out of the ordinary, I want to know right away."

"Already told the boys to ride out in pairs for the next few days. If it is wolves, we might catch a sign. But if it's something else . . ." Jake didn't finish the thought.

"You did right. Did you dispose of the carcasses?"

Jake nodded. "Yeah. No signs of disease, so we dragged 'em out to the ravine east of the ridge. Close to that grizzly kill a couple years back." With that, he set his hat back on his head and gave a brief nod before slipping out the door.

William stood there for a beat, then let himself sink into the leather chair beside the desk, elbows resting on his knees.

Trouble came in threes, some folks said. He wasn't superstitious. His trust rested in the Almighty. Still, with a missing stone and two dead animals on the same day, he couldn't help but wonder—

Was something else waiting just around the corner?

Chapter Seven

As he did every other morning of the week, William rose on Saturday well before sunrise. Breakfast was still more than two hours off, but no matter how early he rose, Mrs. Adler and Chuck —working in tandem—always had coffee waiting for him when he stepped into the kitchen. Neither of them ever appeared at that hour, but the pot was there, hot and full, as if it had prepared itself.

Cradling a steaming mug in his hands, he made his way to the study. There, he lit the oil lamp, settled into the well-worn leather chair near the hearth—cold now from the night—and opened his Bible. The familiar weight of it in his lap brought a quiet comfort. He'd learned years ago that beginning the day in the Word of God didn't keep life's storms from coming, but it kept him anchored when they hit. Though buffeted, he would not be ruined.

A chuckle rumbled in his chest at the image his mind supplied: him blown clean out of the saddle by a gust of wind, cartwheeling down the road toward Gibeon. He suspected the Lord might find that picture just as amusing. Some folks imagined God as a grim judge, always looking for reasons to rebuke or punish. But William had never seen Him that way. The God he knew was full of grace and compassion. A Father who rejoiced over His children with singing. Yes, He judged the wicked, but He was slow to anger and mighty to save. So mighty, He'd sent His only Son to redeem the lost.

Exhaling, William sobered. He adjusted the Bible on his knees and turned the pages with care. The thin leaves rustled softly, yielding with the familiar give of long use. The gilt edges had long since dulled, feathered by years of reading. A corner near the middle curled slightly, worn down by repeated returns to the same passage. He didn't have to look to know the Bible had fallen open to Psalms again. The spine always found its way there.

Faint pencil underlinings whispered of past lessons learned, verses that had offered comfort, correction, or the reminder of God's promises. He brushed one page with the back of his knuckles. Every crease, every smudge, every softened edge bore witness to his journey with the Lord. This wasn't just a book. It was a companion. A testament to the years he'd walked with his Master— through grief and joy, loss and renewal.

After a time, he turned to the beginning. All the way back to Genesis 1:1. *In the beginning God created the heaven and the earth.* Familiar words. Sacred. Solid.

He read slowly, his finger tracing the lines down the columns, taking in again the unfolding story of creation. He moved forward, past the shaping of sea and sky, past the garden, until he came to the eighteenth verse of the second chapter.

And the Lord God said, It is not good that the man should be alone; I will make him an help meet for him.

William stilled.

He read the verse again.

God had created animals, birds, and the creatures of the sea. But for Adam, none was suitable. And so, from the man's own side, the Lord had fashioned the woman to live beside him.

A tightness pinched his chest. That quiet ache again.

He bowed his head. "Father, teach me to be content in all circumstances, as Paul was. I came back to Eden's Gate believing this is where You wanted me. And I've tried to live faithful to that calling. It hasn't always been easy, but You've never forsaken me. That I know." He paused, the weight of unspoken words thick in the air. "Still . . . lately . . ." He let the prayer fade into silence.

And then, without warning, memory returned—an orchestra playing from a high balcony, the swell of a waltz filling a grand ballroom, and the glitter of candlelight reflecting off polished floors. He closed his eyes and saw himself, barely twenty-two, turning beneath a chandelier with Violet Van Tress in his arms.

She'd been eighteen. Beautiful, poised, full of youthful fire and ambition. When she looked at him, he felt ten feet tall and indestructible. He'd thought it was love. The kind that would last forever. The kind Shakespeare had written sonnets about. He had pictured a life with her far from New York. Right here at Eden's Gate. Wide skies, open land, a beautiful home, and cattle dotting the countryside. He thought she would learn to love the land the way he did.

But none of it was what Violet wanted. Not the land nor the life. Nor him.

He shook his head, trying to chase away the lingering strains of music and the aching echo of memory. It had been twelve years. Whatever feelings he'd once carried had long turned to dust. Still, he couldn't help but wonder: Was she married now? Did she have children? Had she found what she was looking for?

The truth was, his love for Violet had died quietly and completely. They'd never been meant to last. Eden's Gate would have suffocated her. And New York had nearly done the same to him.

Even so, the house was quiet these days. Too quiet. He didn't mind solitude most of the time, but lately— especially lately—it clung to him like a second skin. He envied Roger and Sebastian in that regard. Not so long ago, all three of them had been bachelors, free and untethered. Now Sebastian was married and a father. Roger, too, had a wife and soon would have a child. They were putting down roots. Building families.

He alone remained by himself.

And even the Good Book said that wasn't how it was meant to be.

Still sleepy-eyed, Keely tied the bow of her apron behind her back, then turned down the oil lamp on the table and stepped outside into the chill of early morning. Faith and begorra, it must be near freezing. She hugged herself, her breath puffing into the dim pre-dawn air, and hurried across the barnyard, boots crunching against the hard-packed earth.

Warmth wrapped around her the moment she stepped into the kitchen. The scent of coffee, sausage, and something sweet greeted her nose.

Mrs. Adler stood near the dining room doorway, tucking her graying hair beneath a starched white cap. "Good morning, Keely."

"Good morning to you, Mrs. Adler."

"Best have yourself a bite to eat." The same words she said every morning.

At the stove, Chuck glanced over his shoulder. "We've got flapjacks and sausage this morning. Sit your-self down."

"Thank you, Mr. Kincaid." Keely slipped into a chair at the worn kitchen table. A moment later, Chuck set a steaming plate in front of her: three golden flapjacks, their edges crisp and glistening with melted butter, and two plump sausages nestled alongside.

She reached for her fork but paused, taken aback by the unfamiliar sight. These "flapjacks," as he called them, were nothing like the potato cakes she'd grown up eating. At home, cakes fried in a pan meant *boxty*—dense and savory, made from grated and mashed potatoes mixed with flour, fried until the edges were crisp and brown. Mam used to serve them with rashers of bacon, some-times a pat of butter if the churn had been kind that week.

"Boxty," her da had once said with pride, "will find a girl a husband faster than her pretty face." She'd laughed then, but the smell of those breakfasts remained with her.

These, though . . . These were soft and sweet-smelling, their browned tops shining in the lamplight. She cut into one, surprised by how easily the fork slid through. The first bite melted on her tongue—warm, rich, and sweet in a way that startled her.

Chuck grinned from the stove. "Not what you're used to, I reckon."

"No, sir. In Ireland, our cakes fried in a pan are made with potatoes. Heavier fare, they are. These . . ." She took another bite, chewing thoughtfully. "These are like eating sunshine."

Mrs. Adler's lips twitched with the hint of a smile. "Best get used to them, girl. On this ranch, flapjacks will be set before you on many a morning. Next time, try 'em with honey or that maple syrup Mr. Kincaid picks up at the mercantile."

Keely nodded and took another bite, letting herself enjoy the strange sweetness. Yes, she could get used to these flapjacks. But no matter how many mornings passed, she would never forget the taste of home. Her mam's *boxty* would stay in her memory forever.

She had just taken the last bite of sausage when Mrs. Adler said briskly, "Best hurry, girl. I hear Mr. William about." With that, the housekeeper vanished through the swinging door to the dining room.

Keely caught only the briefest glimpse of her employer—just a flash of his shirt sleeve—before the door swung shut again. A surprising flicker of disappointment stirred in her chest. She would've liked to see him this morning, just for a moment. Just to offer a polite greeting.

Daft thought, that.

She rose from the table. No business pining for conversation with the master of the house. Still, the feeling lingered like the last trace of warmth on her plate.

Chapter Eight

Late that morning, with the temperature finally creeping close to fifty degrees, William rested an arm on the top rail of the corral, watching Logan Coe put a three-year-old filly named Sage through her paces. The young mare moved with lithe precision, her coat the muted gray-brown of sun-dried sagebrush, her mane and tail black as ink. William had always favored the grullo coloring, and this one stirred that fondness anew. She wouldn't unseat Skunk in his affections—nothing could—but she might come close. Compact and quick on her feet, she already reined like a dream for her age.

From behind him came a sharp, startled voice. "No! I'll be having nothing for the likes of you. Get down!"

He turned at once, recognizing the Irish lilt. Keely Boyle stood across the barnyard, her arms raised high above her head, a wicker laundry basket clutched in her hands. Rowdy, one of the younger ranch dogs—a brown-and-white pup still growing into himself, all legs and too-big paws—danced in circles around her, leaping up to investigate the mysterious treasure she carried. Two other dogs, Old Blue and Jock—retired from their ranch duties —lifted their heads from where they lay in the shade to see if there was anything of interest. Finding none, they ignored the youngster's antics and lowered their heads again.

"Rowdy!" William called sharply, stepping away from the fence. "No!"

The pup dropped flat to the ground mid-leap, tail thumping as his master approached.

William reached them in a few strides. "What have you got there?"

"Laundry for the line, sir. Sure and there's nothing in here he'd want to eat."

"You hear that, Rowdy?" He leaned low and gave the dog's head a brisk pat. "Nothing for you." He straightened and reached for the basket. "Here. Let me help you with that. It looks heavy."

"'Tis no heavier than what I'm used to, sir." Her hands hesitated on the handles, but after a moment's pause, she allowed him to take it.

He turned toward the clotheslines stretched across the grassy area near the southwest side of the house. The lines stood well away from the corral, far enough to avoid the worst of the dust stirred up by horses or wind.

Keely hurried after him, voice lowered with worry. "This is my work, sir. Mrs. Adler won't like it if she thinks I'm interruptin' your morning."

"Don't worry about Mrs. Adler." He set the basket on the ground. "If she says anything, I'll set her straight."

A damp, clean scent rose from the pile of freshly washed clothes. William reached for a shirt, its weight heavy and wet in his hands.

Keely stepped closer, cheeks flushed. "Best shake it out first, sir. Else it'll dry wrinkled."

He glanced at her, one brow raised. "I've hung a shirt or two in my life."

"Not shirts that needed to look proper come Sunday, I'll wager." She took the shirt from him and gave it a brisk, practiced shake, sending droplets flying.

He smiled faintly and reached for a sheet. The wind caught it as he flung it over the line, snapping the fabric like a sail. The sound, the sun overhead, the rhythm of an ordinary day. It all felt incredibly satisfying.

Keely tilted her head, assessing his work with a slight smile. "A fair enough job, I suppose."

"High praise," he said, his tone dry but amused. There was something about earning her approval that pleased him more than it should have. He picked up one of his work shirts. "This one. How do you want it done?"

"By the shoulders," she answered quickly, demonstrating with the shirt in her hands. "If you hang it by the hem, the collar will dry crooked, and I'll be longer with the iron." She held out her hand. "But here. Let me have it. 'Tis not right when you're payin' me to do the work."

He handed it over without protest, watching as she stood on her toes to pin the garment in place. A strand of her hair had slipped free, catching sunlight like copper thread. She brushed it away with the back of her wrist, focused entirely on her task.

William remained still, basket forgotten, content to

observe the quiet rhythm of her work. The sheet flapped beside them, and the shirts fluttered gently, catching the spring sunlight. And Keely—this slight young woman with careful hands and a troubled past—fit into the scene with surprising ease.

"You don't have to call me 'sir' all the time," he said after a beat. "Makes me sound older than I am."

She froze for the barest second, then continued pinning the shirt. "But you're the master of Eden's Gate."

"It's William." It surprised him how much he wanted her to say it. "Just William."

She flicked a glance at him, uncertain. A pause stretched between them, and then softly, as if testing the weight of it, she repeated, "William." Her eyes dropped quickly, and she bent over the basket for another sheet.

He smiled to himself, the sound of his name on her lips lingering in his ears longer than it should. As he turned and strode back toward the corral, he felt lighter somehow, buoyed by sunlight, by the snap of clean linens in the breeze, and by the quiet promise that maybe, just maybe, something new had begun.

Keely stood still for a moment, the sound of his name still warm on her tongue.

William.

What was she thinking, calling him that? He was the master of this ranch, and she was a housemaid. A girl who'd come with little more than the clothes on her back and secrets in her heart. She had no right to speak his name with such familiarity, let alone feel the faint thrill that had risen when she'd said it.

The wind stirred the linen beside her, billowing it wide before she pinned it in place. Her fingers stung from the morning's scrubbing, raw from lye soap and hot water. Laundry day always left her aching and bone-weary, but the ache was familiar. Back at Hooke Manor, there had been a small army of housemaids to share the burden, plus a laundry maid whose only duty was to wash and press from one week's end to the next. Keely was often grateful that she didn't have to work at that post, even though the housekeeper still criticized her harshly if a hem sagged or a cuff had the slightest yellow tinge.

Here, things were different. There were fewer hands, fewer rules, and fewer eyes watching her every move. The linens she washed belonged to a man who'd carried her basket without a word of reproach. A man who'd offered help instead of scorn. That had never happened at the manor. Not once. Lords did not hang sheets in the sun.

She bent to lift one of his shirts—heavy, damp, the cotton cool in her hands. She smoothed it across the line, pinned it carefully by the shoulders, and stepped back, satisfied to see it hanging clean and straight. A smile tugged at her lips. Whatever else Eden's Gate might ask of her, she could at least keep the laundry line a picture of order.

A shout turned her head toward the corral.

William had swapped places with the ranch hand—

Logan Coe, she remembered—and now sat astride the gray-brown filly. Keely rested one hand on the edge of the basket, shading her eyes with the other as she watched. The mare darted left, quick as a startled bird, but William moved with her, seat steady, posture relaxed. He spoke to the filly, his voice soft, low, calm. She couldn't make out the words, but the tone was unmistakable. Gentle. Assured.

The horse flicked an ear toward him, testing his intent. In the next breath, they moved together, two beings reading each other with ease.

Keely's breath caught as she watched.

There was strength in him, yes, but not the cruel kind. Not the sharp edge of dominance that so many men wielded as if it were their birthright. William Overstreet had authority, but it came wrapped in something quieter. Patience. Kindness. A steadiness that felt more like shelter than threat.

She turned back to her work and lifted a towel from the basket, trying to push the thoughts from her mind. Still, her gaze slipped again and again toward the corral, drawn to the sight of him, confident in the saddle, his movements fluid, his posture sure.

With the last of the day's washing pinned on the line and drying in the sun, Keely balanced the basket against her hip and turned toward the corral for one last glance.

William had dismounted while her back was turned and was now stripping the saddle from the filly's damp back. His hat lay forgotten on the ground, and without it, the tousled waves of his hair caught the sun. His face was clearer now—unshadowed, strong, and, to her dismay, entirely too handsome.

"William," she whispered, almost without thinking.

And then she froze. Her eyes widened. Sweet sufferin' cats! What was wrong with her? Had she taken complete leave of her senses? She couldn't let herself think about him in that way. It was foolishness of the worst sort.

Wasn't it bad enough she'd once followed another man across an ocean—even knowing he didn't love her? Falling for William Overstreet would be worse. Far worse. He was her employer. He was kind, yes. Generous, too. But a man like him would never look twice at a girl like her. Not really. And she couldn't afford to let her heart get tangled up.

Tugging the basket higher on her hip, Keely ducked her head and turned away from the corral. Her steps quickened, the hem of her skirt swishing at her ankles as she made her way toward the house.

She didn't look back.

"She's a pretty thing," Logan said just before the back door thudded shut behind Keely.

William's jaw tightened as he ran the brush along Sage's spine. The filly shifted slightly, then settled again under the gentle strokes.

The cowboy wasn't wrong. Anyone with working eyes could see that Keely was more than just pretty. That wild tumble of red hair. Those luminous green eyes. She stood out to William in a way no woman had in a long time. Perhaps ever. But hearing another man say it—and so casually—rubbed him the wrong way.

"I wouldn't mind getting to know her better," Logan added.

William turned a sharp look on the younger man. "You've got colts to break. Don't waste your time mooning over the housemaid."

The young man drew back a step. "Meant nothing by it, boss. Just saying she's easy on the eyes."

He didn't answer. Instead, he tossed the brush onto the nearby ledge, grabbed the saddle and blanket from the rail, and headed for the tack room. His boots scuffed against the barn floor, his temper rising with every step.

Logan had meant no harm. He knew that. The boy had just spoken what every other hand on Eden's Gate was probably already thinking. Keely was beautiful. And young. And new. She was bound to turn heads.

But it didn't sit right with him all the same.

He reached the tack room, shoved open the door, and dropped the saddle onto the rack harder than necessary. The leather creaked. He stood there a moment, staring at the saddle, willing himself to shake off the tension coiling in his shoulders.

He'd hired Keely out of a desire to help. She'd looked scared half to death when he met her, and he'd seen something familiar in that fear. Something that stirred memories he'd rather not revisit. Giving her a job, offering her a place to land, had felt like the right thing to do.

But now . . . if all the men on the ranch started sniffing around, hoping for more than polite conversation, it would complicate everything. She deserved peace. Safety. Not the scrutiny of a bunch of ranch hands, each wondering if they had a shot.

His jaw clenched again. He'd need to have a word with the men. Set some boundaries. Make it clear Keely was to be treated with respect—and left alone.

A question slipped in unbidden. *To all except me?* The thought stopped him cold.

He stared at the saddle as if it had betrayed him. Where in blazes had that come from?

Keely was lovely, sure. She had a quiet, capable strength and a rare kind of softness in her eyes. But she worked under his roof. He wasn't about to become one of those men who took advantage of power or proximity.

His reaction was nothing more than instinct. A natural response of a man to a beautiful woman.

Nothing more.

And yet . . .

The thought of Logan—or any of the others—getting close to her riled him in a way he couldn't easily dismiss. That wasn't instinct. That wasn't a passing interest.

It was something else entirely.

William exhaled hard through his nose, pushed off the saddle rack, and stepped back into the light.

He had work to do. And the last thing he needed was to complicate his life by falling for the woman who hung out his laundry to dry.

Chapter Nine

It was on a Wednesday morning, three weeks after Keely's arrival at Eden's Gate, that Mrs. Adler made a surprising suggestion over breakfast. "You should take the buggy into town today and fetch a few supplies."

Keely froze, her fork midway to her mouth. "Sure and I wouldn't know how."

Mrs. Adler arched an eyebrow. "You've been to Gibeon for church the last three Sundays. Don't tell me you don't know the way. It's a straight shot, hardly room to get lost, even for a newcomer."

"That's not what I meant, ma'am. 'Tis the horse I'm worried about. I've never driven a buggy before. Never held a pair of reins in me life. Not once."

"Well, then." The housekeeper planted her fists on her hips. "That won't do. You can't live on a ranch and be helpless that way. No, it simply won't do." And with that, she swept out of the kitchen.

Keely looked toward Chuck, who stood at the stove, flipping flapjacks. "What do you suppose she's meanin' to do, Mr. Kincaid?"

He chuckled. "Heaven only knows. But when she gets a bee in her bonnet, best clear the path."

Keely didn't have long to wait for her answer. A few hours later, she found herself in the barnyard beside Logan Coe, watching and listening as he explained the intricacies of harnessing a horse to a buggy.

"Duke here's a good old soul," the cowboy said, patting the gelding's neck with affection. "Won't give you trouble. He'd rather plod than run, truth be told, which is just fine while you're learning."

Plodding sounded fine to her, too. The thought of holding reins and steering that much horseflesh with nothing but leather straps was enough to make her palms sweat.

"First thing to know," Logan continued, "never sneak up behind a horse. Let him see and hear you coming. Talk to him. Steady and soft. Helps him know you're a friend."

Keely swallowed and edged toward Duke's shoulder. "Good morning to you, Duke," she said, her voice gentle but wary, like she was greeting someone who might take offense.

"That's it." Logan handed her a halter. "Now, slip this over his head. Go on. Don't be shy."

Her fingers shook as she lifted the leather. But Duke lowered his head obligingly, and after a few fumbling tries, she got the buckle fastened.

"There you go. Not so bad, was it?" Logan grinned. "Now, he needs a brushing before we tack him up. Dirt under leather'll rub him raw." He offered her a currycomb.

She brushed the horse's shoulder tentatively.

"Not so gentle, Miss Boyle. Firm, like scrubbin' a pot clean."

A reluctant laugh escaped her. "A pot I can manage." She pressed harder. Duke swished his tail, but whether in pleasure or protest, she couldn't say.

"Better. Now here's the pad. Goes right behind the withers."

Withers. That was a new one. But before she could ask, Logan positioned it for her and guided her hands. "Right here. Even. Not too far forward."

She nodded, biting her lip in concentration.

"Next is the harness saddle." He lifted the heavier piece onto Duke's back. "Now fasten the girth under his belly. Snug, but not tight enough to pinch."

Keely crouched to reach beneath the horse's middle, and Rowdy—who had become her canine shadow in recent days—ran over to see what had drawn her attention. But when Duke shifted his weight, both she and the dog jumped back.

Logan chuckled. "He's just settling his feet. Try again. Slide your hand between the strap and him to check it. If your hand fits, you've got it right."

"Stay, Rowdy," she commanded before trying again. "Like this?"

"Perfect, miss."

The quiet praise straightened her spine a little.

"Now for the bridle. Guide the bit in gentle. Don't bang his teeth."

She hesitated, then took it from him. With Logan advising her from the other side of the horse, Duke accepted the bit with an easy patience that surprised her.

"Well now. Look at you, miss. Wouldn't know it was your first time."

She smiled faintly. "He's making it easy on me, I'm thinkin'."

"That's Duke for you." Logan threaded the long leather reins through the rings on the harness saddle. "These are your lines. They guide him. Just remember. Don't yank. Ask."

"Ask?"

"Sure." He nodded. "Horse listens better when you ask than when you demand." He led Duke between the buggy shafts. "Mind his feet. You want to keep your toes."

Keely stepped back quickly.

Logan fastened the shafts to the harness, then clipped the traces to what he called the singletree. "These take the pull. Without 'em, you'd be going nowhere." Finally, he stepped back, scanning his work. "Always walk 'round and check every buckle. Better to take a minute now than chase down a runaway later."

"Runaway?" Her hands flew to the dark cotton apron tied snugly at her waist, fingers worrying the sturdy fabric. "'Tis a wonder I'll ever remember it all."

Logan grinned. "Give it time, Miss Boyle. One of these days, you'll be hitching up quicker than me."

Saints preserve them. She doubted that was true.

The sound of approaching horses drew their attention. William and two ranch hands—Tom Flores and Rocky Turner—rode into the yard. The men dismounted and tied their horses to the hitching post. Tom and Rocky made for the bunkhouse, while William headed straight toward her.

"What's all this?" he asked, curiosity lacing his tone.

"Mrs. Adler asked me to teach Miss Boyle how to hitch a horse to a rig," Logan said. "Gotta learn to drive it too. That's next."

William raised an eyebrow.

Keely rushed to explain. "Mrs. Adler wanted me to go into town for some supplies, sir. But I . . . I've never driven a buggy before. She was saying that isn't a good thing on a ranch."

He was quiet for a moment, then nodded. "She's right about that." He turned to Logan. "I'll take it from here. You've got other chores, don't you?"

"Yes, sir." Logan tipped his hat. Then, with a cheeky grin tossed her way, he added, "Have fun, Miss Boyle."

Keely managed a tight smile, but her insides quivered. *Fun?* She doubted that very much.

William watched Logan saunter off, his grin as cocky as ever, and felt a flicker of irritation. Why had Mrs. Adler assigned him to teach Keely how to drive a buggy? Surely one of the older hands would've made a more suitable instructor.

He turned back to Keely. She stood rigid beside the buggy, her hands folded neatly before her apron, eyes wary beneath a furrowed brow. Pretty, he couldn't help thinking, then pushed the thought aside. Best not to let such notions linger in his mind again.

"Well then," he said, adopting a brisk tone. "If you're going to drive into Gibeon, fastening straps isn't the only thing you'll need to know."

"That's what I was fearing."

A smile tugged at one corner of his mouth. She had the courage to face down a new life in a new land, yet a placid gelding and a buggy had her near trembling. He admired that sort of honesty.

"Climb on up." He nodded toward the buggy seat. "You'll do the driving. I'll be beside you."

Her eyes flew to his. "You, sir?"

"Me." He kept his voice steady, though something stirred in him at the thought of sitting beside her. "Don't worry. Duke won't run off. And I won't let anything happen to you."

She nodded, turning toward the buggy and placing a hand on the side rail.

"Wait," he said. "If Mrs. Adler needs something from town, we might as well see to it while you're learning. I'll find out what she's after. Wait here."

He found the housekeeper in the front parlor, polishing the sideboard with brisk, efficient strokes. "Mrs. Adler, I'm taking Miss Boyle into town in the buggy. She said there were supplies you needed?"

"You're taking her?"

"She needs driving lessons, doesn't she?"

"Well, yes, Mr. William, but I thought Logan—"

"Logan has other work."

She gave him a long, unreadable look. "Hmm."

"Do you have a list?"

"I do. Just a moment." She disappeared into the kitchen, returning with a slip of paper. "There. A few things we're low on."

"Thanks." He tucked the note into his coat pocket.

"Might as well eat something before you go. It'll be a while before you're back."

"If we're famished, we can grab a bite at Miss Irene's while we're in town."

She sniffed. "Waste of good money."

He tugged the brim of his hat lower over his brow. "Back in a few hours, if all goes well."

Keely was still waiting in the barnyard, looking no less nervous than before, Rowdy pressed up close against her skirt, as if to offer reassurance.

William walked to her and offered his hand. "We're ready."

She hesitated just a second before accepting it. Her fingers were cool in his palm, her grip light but steady.

"Get back, Rowdy," he said to the dog as he helped Keely onto the seat. Then he stepped up beside her, gathered the reins, and placed them carefully into her hands. "Do you have gloves?"

"Yes, sir. Mrs. Adler made sure I did." She returned the reins to his hands, pulled the gloves from her apron pocket, and tugged them on.

"Good," he said. "First lesson. Hold the reins firm, but not tight. Duke'll listen if you ask him right."

She gripped the leather as if afraid the reins would wriggle away.

"Easy. Feel the weight of them. Duke's mouth is on the other end. Don't jerk."

She adjusted her grip, easing the tension in her arms.

"Better. Now give him a cluck with your tongue and a light shake of the reins."

She did, hesitantly. Duke flicked his ears and moved forward without protest.

She gasped.

William chuckled low in his throat. "See? He's doing the work. You're just guiding him."

The buggy rolled across the barnyard and around the side of the barn. He kept a watchful eye on the gelding, but Duke behaved as expected—calm, steady, unhurried.

Keely sat straight as a post, her eyes locked ahead.

"Breathe, Miss Boyle. You're safe."

She spared him a glance, the corner of her mouth twitching as if she wanted to argue but didn't dare lose her focus.

The sun was warm on their backs, and the spring air held a hint of sage and greening fields. The road unspooled ahead of them like a ribbon, weaving gently between stretches of pale grass.

"If you lay the right rein against his neck, soft and easy, he'll turn left. Try it."

She did as instructed. Duke shifted obligingly, veering toward the left side of the road. A spark of wonder flared in her eyes, chasing out the fear.

"There you go," William said. "Not so hard, is it?"

She didn't answer at once, but her smile—small and shy—was genuine. And it did something to him.

He turned his attention back to the road, jaw tightening slightly. Teaching her was practical. Necessary. Nothing more.

At least, that's what he kept telling himself.

Chapter Ten

The trip into Gibeon that day seemed to take ten times longer than Keely's previous three journeys for Sunday services.

Was it the day of the week? Of course not.

Daft thought.

She knew the reason, and he sat right beside her.

"Look ahead, Miss Boyle," William said, breaking into her thoughts. "You've made it to town." He pointed. "Take Duke over to the Teton General Store, then ease back on the reins. Nice and slow. He'll know where to stop. He's done it plenty of times."

Following his guidance, she laid the right rein gently along Duke's neck. As they neared the mercantile, she pulled back on the reins, just as he'd taught her. The gelding came to a halt a few feet shy of the hitching post.

"You didn't need me at all, Miss Boyle."

"Sure and that's not the truth."

He jumped down from the buggy with practiced

ease, then turned and offered her a hand, helping her descend with care, as if she were made of glass.

"We'll leave the list with Mrs. Hathaway," he said. "While she gathers the supplies, we can have a look at Roger's studio. See what he's been up to."

How easily these Americans mixed with one another. She was his housemaid—paid to clean his floors and dust his bookshelves—and yet here he was, standing beside her on the boardwalk like they were of equal station. Such a thing would never have happened back in Ireland. Or England. She'd known her place there. Not the lowest, but low enough. Her only brush with climbing above it had been her foolish infatuation with Roger Bernhardt. But he had never belonged to the gentry, despite his friendship with the earl. Roger came from the merchant class, a rung or two above her own.

But William Overstreet. How would she classify him?

He wasn't gentry. No inherited title, no centuries-old estate. And he certainly wasn't a merchant, selling goods behind a shop counter. Yet he owned thousands of acres. Land stretching beyond the horizon. Cattle enough to make him a wealthy man. In England, such holdings might have nudged him near the landed gentry, if only he'd been born into it.

"Wait here," he said. "I won't be long."

She watched him go into the general store, her thoughts still turning. There was something about him that unsettled all her notions of class. His speech was plain, his manner unadorned. His skin was sun-darkened, his hands rough from work. And yet, he carried himself with quiet authority, with a command no butler could imitate and no nobleman could lend. He was the master here. Not just by title, but by his presence. And every man on Eden's Gate and here in Gibeon knew it.

Her thoughts tumbling, she smoothed the front of her new skirt, the one she'd made—along with her new blouse—from the fabric Mrs. Adler had provided a few weeks before.

Maybe America had its own classes. Not by blood, but by something else. Something earned. Maybe a rancher here could stand higher than a lord back home and bow to none of England's rules.

Was it possible he didn't see her as lesser, simply because she was Irish and a housemaid?

That question still lingered when William emerged from the store, his eyes meeting hers, his smile unguarded.

Her pulse fluttered. *Sweet sufferin' cats!*

"All right," he said, coming to her side. "Let's check out this new gallery of Roger's." He turned toward the boardwalk, took one stride, then glanced back to wait for her.

And so she joined him.

In her previous visits to Gibeon for Sunday services, she'd seen only the edge of town from the church. But now, walking west along the wooden walkway, she took in the full length of Main Street, its boardwalks lined with shops and signs. Everything she saw interested her, and if she'd been alone, she would have stopped at every window to discover what was within.

At last, they came to a building with freshly painted trim and a sign in the window: Bernhardt Art Gallery.

William stepped ahead and opened the door, causing a little bell overhead to jingle. "Miss Boyle," he said, motioning her in.

Keely moved into the gallery, her eyes widening. The high ceiling gave the space an airy feel, and the white-washed walls made it seem flooded with light. Paintings hung in even intervals—oil and watercolor, large and small, some framed, others bare canvas stretched tight. Most were of landscapes, wild creatures, mountain vistas, quiet streams. Scenes that felt alive, places that called to be stepped into.

"Would you look at that now," she whispered. "Isn't it grand?"

William came to stand beside her. "It is indeed."

From a doorway at the back, Roger's voice called out, "I shall be only a moment."

"No hurry," William replied. "It's just us."

Just us. The words rippled through her like a pebble dropped in still water.

Roger appeared moments later, wiping his hands on a paint-streaked cloth. "Well now," he said with a smile. "Didn't expect to see you in town on a weekday."

"Mrs. Adler needed supplies," William explained. "And Miss Boyle needed a driving lesson. We thought we'd kill two birds with one stone."

"Is that so?" Roger turned his attention to Keely. "Learning to drive a buggy will serve you well here."

William turned slowly, eyes scanning the walls. "The place looks amazing, my friend."

"I have Victoria to thank for that. She keeps me from cluttering the space so the paintings can breathe."

"Excellent decision."

"I'm learning that things usually go better when I listen to her."

William chuckled. "No doubt."

As the two men talked, Keely drifted toward one of the smaller paintings. A watercolor. The colors—soft and familiar—drew her in. When she stepped closer, her breath caught. She knew this place.

Fenwicke. A small English village nestled just outside the Hooke Manor estate. The church steeple, the row of narrow cottages with thatched roofs, the tiny bridge over the brook. All of it lovingly rendered in delicate brush-strokes.

A lump rose in her throat. Home. Or what she'd once imagined home might be. Not a place she'd truly possessed, but one she'd longed for.

William came up beside her. "By golly," he said, peering at the painting. "That's a typical English village if ever I've seen one."

"'Tis Fenwicke."

He tilted his head. "The village near Hooke Manor?"

"Yes."

"Ah. I never saw the manor or its village." He glanced back toward Roger. "You were there often, weren't you?"

Roger answered from across the room, "As often as I could get away from London."

Keely reached out, her fingertips brushing the edge of the simple wooden frame. The painting stirred something deep in her, something tender and aching. She hadn't just left a country. She'd left every hope she'd ever tied to that village, to that manor, to the possibility of belonging somewhere.

Now she stood between two men—one who had been a dream, and one who was feeling far more real.

Something in Keely's expression as she stood gazing at the painting—her eyes distant, her features touched with longing—made William decide to give her a few moments alone. He turned and strolled along the back wall of the gallery, pausing before each painting. He admired Roger's work, but his thoughts remained tethered to the Irish miss behind him.

A few moments later, Roger joined him. In a low voice, he said, "Keely seems a little sad. Something wrong?"

He glanced over his shoulder. "She seemed fine on the trip to town. I think it's that painting she's looking at. Might've stirred up homesickness."

Roger hummed softly in understanding.

William shifted his weight. "We're going to eat at Miss Irene's before heading back to Eden's Gate. If you haven't eaten yet, I'd be glad if you and Victoria joined us. Might do Keely some good."

"That sounds delightful. I'll go to the house to get Victoria, and we'll meet you there."

William nodded and returned to where Keely still stood, her eyes still fixed on the watercolor. He saw a flicker of movement in her lashes as he approached, and when he said her name, she turned to meet his gaze. But it seemed to him that it took a few seconds longer for all of her to come back to the present.

"Let's go get something to eat," he said gently. "Have you met Irene Sullivan?"

"No, sir."

"Well, it's time you did. You'll like her."

He offered his arm, but she stared at it like it might bite her. For a brief second, the rebuff stung. Then he remembered the rigid rules of class in her home country. Of course, she would hesitate. A housemaid didn't walk arm-in-arm with her employer, not in private nor in public. Taking pity on her discomfort, he gestured toward the door instead.

As they exited, he called back over his shoulder, "See you there, Roger."

The door shut behind them, and they followed the boardwalk back down Main Street, the clatter of wagons and murmuring voices threading through the warm midday air.

After a prolonged silence, William asked, "Did you go into Fenwicke often?"

She looked up at him. "Me? No, sir. Not often."

"Why not? It was nearby, wasn't it?"

"Oh, aye. It was an easy walk. But me duties kept me at the manor, and I wasn't the sort they sent to buy things in the shops."

"Why not?"

She hesitated. "I was only a housemaid," she said quietly. "And I'm Irish."

William absorbed her words without comment, though he felt a heaviness settle in his chest. He wasn't unfamiliar with the deep-rooted prejudice against the Irish. In England, people had feared Catholic influence for centuries. The so-called "Irish question" dominated political conversation, and the disdain he'd witnessed among the Eton set—sons mimicking their fathers' sneering contempt—was hard to forget, even more than a decade later.

America had its share of ugliness too. In the big cities of the East, signs had once openly declared: No Irish Need Apply. Even out West, in the mining towns and rail camps, old hatreds died hard. But on ranches like Eden's Gate and in places like Gibeon, William had seen something different. Here, hard work mattered more than lineage. Skill and integrity counted more than accent or ancestry. And he hoped that would prove true for Keely.

As they crossed the street, he slowed his stride so she could keep pace, her skirt hem brushing the dust of the road. The shadow of melancholy still lingered on her face, though she kept her chin up, surveying the town as if determined not to let it conquer her.

The restaurant windows gleamed with sunlight, reflecting the sky so brightly they had to squint as they climbed onto the boardwalk. A painted sign above the door proclaimed Miss Irene's. From within, the savory scent of roasted beef and onions drifted out when the door swung open.

"After you, Miss Boyle." William held the door.

She stepped inside. The room was bright and neat, full of simple charm. White curtains trimmed with lace framed the windows. Each table wore a crisp linen cloth, with small jars of wildflowers placed in the center. The indistinct hum of conversation and the gentle clink of cutlery filled the air.

Irene Sullivan approached them with a smile. A woman in her forties, she had keen, perceptive eyes and a straightforward manner. Her dark red hair—several shades deeper than Keely's—was tucked beneath a white cap. Her apron bore signs of a busy lunch hour.

"Mr. Overstreet," she said warmly. "Rarely see you in my little establishment."

"Not often, Miss Irene, but always a pleasure to come in when I'm able."

Her gaze shifted to Keely.

William gestured. "This is Miss Keely Boyle. She's working with Mrs. Adler at Eden's Gate."

The warmth in Irene's expression deepened. "A pleasure, Miss Boyle. And if you're the reason this one's decided to come in and eat, then you're doubly welcome."

Color rose in Keely's cheeks. "Thank you, ma'am."

The front door opened, and Roger entered with Victoria on his arm. His affable grin appeared the moment he spotted them. "We're not too late, I hope?"

"Right on time," William replied. "We only just sat down."

Irene motioned toward the chalkboard near the door. "Today's special is still hot. I'll give you a minute to settle in, then come back for your order."

As Roger and Victoria crossed the room to join them, William glanced at Keely. Something had shifted in her expression. The shadow in her eyes had lightened. Perhaps it was the presence of another woman that eased her spirits.

Whatever the reason, her faint smile made something tight inside William release. He hadn't brought her to town to fill her with nostalgia nor to cheer her up. But he was thankful for the result all the same.

Chapter Eleven

I
t took some getting used to, day after day of blue skies without a single rain cloud in sight. Not that Keely was complaining.

"Sure and I'm used to it now," she said aloud, lifting her face to the morning sun on that mild Saturday in May.

An hour earlier, Mrs. Adler had shooed her out of the house. "Go on with you. You deserve a bit of time to yourself. Take a walk and have a gander about the ranch. You've hardly stepped outside the barnyard these past weeks, not counting Sunday services in Gibeon."

"But me chores," Keely had protested.

"There's nothing that can't wait till Monday. Go. It'll do you good."

And so here she was—alone, having commanded Rowdy to stay behind—wandering alongside a swift-running stream, the scent of clean earth and new grass rising on the breeze. The land rolled eastward, green and waking to spring, and her gaze followed it. Though she might have grown used to the unchanging blue of the Idaho sky, there was no getting used to those towering mountains in the distance. Not truly. They stirred something in her spirit every time she looked at them, something too big to name.

From a far-off corner of memory came her mam's voice: *"I will lift up mine eyes unto the hills, from whence cometh my help."*

She stopped walking. "Oh, Mam," she whispered, a lump rising in her throat. "You never saw the like o' these hills."

"My help cometh from the Lord, which made heaven and earth."

Tears gathered without warning. "I wish you could be here with me, Mam. Sure and I do. You would love everything about this land."

Sniffling, she wiped her eyes with the side of her hand, then pressed on, letting the gentle hush wrap around her. Warm sun met the lingering cool of morning, and now and again a breeze stirred the tall grasses, brushing past her ankles. Birds chirped here and there, but otherwise, the land lay quiet and still.

Until, perhaps half an hour later, the silence changed.

At first she thought the wind was playing tricks on her ears, carrying a strange hum across the grass. Then she caught it again—low, steady notes rising here and there. A deep-chested murmur that lingered in the air. Every so often, one voice broke away, longer and louder, before settling back into the lazy rhythm of the rest.

Faith and begorra! What was it she heard?

She crested a rise, the slope steeper than it first

appeared, and at the top, she found her answer. Cattle. An entire company of them, their lowing rolling across the pasture as they tore mouthfuls of grass and chewed with patient determination. The sight and sound of them stopped her in her tracks.

Back in Ireland, her only knowledge of such animals had come from the scrawny milk cow tethered behind her mam's cottage. But these were different animals entirely.

Big, broad-shouldered beasts, their hides a rich, ruddy red, with stark white faces so clean they looked painted on. Even their chests, bellies, and legs wore the same bright white. At first glance they looked comical, but the longer she watched, the more she saw strength in them—strength and patience. They moved deliberately, heads low, tails swishing, grazing without hurry.

They belonged to this land, just like the sagebrush and the mountains. They fit here. Unlike her, perhaps. But she pushed the thought away.

Turning a quarter to the right, her gaze caught on a gleam in the distance, a shimmer of light on water. A pond, she guessed. What the cowboys called a watering hole. No cattle gathered there now, but a man on horseback had just ridden up to it and dismounted. He knelt beside the edge, then stood a moment later and swung back into the saddle.

From this distance, she couldn't say who it was. Still, she watched closely. His movements were sure, practiced. He turned his horse in the opposite direction from the ranch house and galloped away, soon disappearing beyond a rise.

A pang of disappointment surprised her. She'd hoped it was William.

"It's daft, you are, Keely Boyle."

She turned away and retraced her steps down the rise, but William remained stubbornly in her thoughts.

It wasn't right. It wasn't wise. Hadn't she learned anything from her foolish infatuation with Roger? She hadn't crossed an ocean to fall into the same trap again. And William Overstreet was no safer a choice than Roger had been. More dangerous, maybe. She could still see his eyes, warm and flecked with gold, and the way his smile crept in slow and easy, like sunlight through shutters.

Sure and you're not here to lose your heart.

She was in America to find her footing. To make a new life and to keep out of trouble.

Falling for the master of Eden's Gate? That would be trouble indeed.

William saw her from a distance.

There was no mistaking that wild red hair. Not with the sunlight glinting off coppery curls. At the ranch, she kept it tucked away under a white cap, and on Sundays, she wore a plain straw bonnet that hid most of it. But now, alone on the open range, the wind made her hair dance.

Good sense told him to turn Skunk toward the ranch house and ride on. But good sense didn't win out.

He nudged the stallion in her direction instead. Toward the creek. Toward Keely.

She spotted him and stopped walking, lifting a hand to shield her eyes. She stood still, waiting, her silhouette framed by light.

Slowing the stallion from a canter to a walk, William called out, "I didn't expect to find you out this far from the house, Miss Boyle. Everything all right?" When he drew close, he reined Skunk to a halt and dismounted.

"Should I not be here?"

"Not at all." He dropped to the ground beside her. "You're welcome to explore as much of the ranch as you like."

She lowered her gaze, but her voice was steady. "'Tis truly beautiful. This land."

So are you, his heart whispered, but he silenced the thought before it reached his lips. "Yes," he said instead, "it is beautiful. I pray I will steward it well."

"Have you lived here always?"

"Not always. But it's where I belong." He glanced at the horizon. "My grandfather started the ranch close to fifty years ago. He passed it on to my mother, and she left it to her children. My sister had other interests. First in New York City, now in England."

Color rose in Keely's cheeks. "Sure and I forget sometimes that her ladyship is your sister."

"'Her ladyship,'" he echoed with quiet amusement, then chuckled. "I have a hard time thinking of her that way."

He saw Jocelyn in his mind's eye—astride a galloping horse, hair flying, hat bouncing against her back. Not a typical aristocrat by any means. Certainly not how one pictured the mother of a future earl.

"She was always kind to me," Keely said softly.

The words drew his gaze back to her. "That's just how she is."

Keely turned away, looking toward the Tetons. Her voice dropped to a near whisper. "I wasn't deserving of her kindness."

William frowned, unsure if he'd heard her right. Why would she say such a thing?

He watched the rise and fall of her shoulders as she drew a slow breath. When she turned back to him, the spark of determination in her eyes was unmistakable. Whatever memory had stirred those words was gone now. Or at least pushed aside.

"Would you like a ride back to the house?" he offered. "I can put you up behind me."

The spark of determination faded into alarm as she looked at the stallion. Her eyes widened. "Will you be giving me riding lessons next?"

He laughed. "I just might. But not today."

"Well, that's something I'll be thankful for, Mr. Overstreet."

William, he wanted to say. He almost did. She'd spoken his name once before, on a laundry day, but not since. Not when he'd taught her to drive the buggy. Not even in town with Roger and Victoria. It shouldn't matter. But it did.

"Come on," he said, a bit more gruffly than intended. "I'll walk with you. I could use the stretch."

He gathered Skunk's reins in one hand and started

walking. As she had in Gibeon, Keely fell into step beside him. Their pace was unhurried, their silence companionable. The tension left his shoulders.

"How far did you walk today?" he asked after a time.

"Far enough to see your great herd of cattle. I've never seen so many in one place."

"There are a lot. And every one of them matters."

"You sound as if you love them."

He let out a short laugh. "I wouldn't say love, exactly. But yes, they matter to me. Like the land, I am responsible for them. I'm responsible for their well-being, and I believe they matter to God."

"But don't you sell them for meat?"

"I do. That's part of ranching. But I don't believe that lessens their worth in the Lord's eyes."

"You'll be sounding like a preacher now."

"I'm not sure Reverend Blankenship would appreciate that comparison." His laughter came easier this time.

Keely smiled. "Me mam had a way of looking at the world, of caring for the wee creatures. She used to say we ought to treasure every bit of God's creation. I'm thinking she would have understood you better than I'm doing."

"I'm sorry I never knew your mother. Sounds like we would've gotten along just fine."

She glanced over at him, and he caught the shimmer of unshed tears in her eyes. "I'll be thinking the same, sir."

He looked ahead toward the creek winding its way through Eden's Gate, its waters catching the light like a silver ribbon. "My father and I never saw eye to eye. He founded Overstreet Shipping and expected me to follow in his footsteps. I tried. After I came back from England, I gave it an honest effort. But I wasn't made for the city. I wanted this." He swept a hand out toward the land. "The air, the space, the rhythm of the seasons."

"And your sister? She stayed behind?"

"She was better suited for our father's world. Jocelyn's always been the one with the head for business. But me? I was meant to ride fences and count cattle. Took a long time for my father to accept that."

Keely nodded slowly. "I saw New York City for meself. I cannot imagine you there."

"Neither can I. Not anymore."

She smiled faintly. "I'd be wantin' this place too, if it were mine."

He thought of Violet again. Strange, how he'd gone years without her crossing his mind. She would have hated Eden's Gate and the isolation. She would have hated the wide open sky and the mountains that towered over the valley. She would have hated the lowing of cattle and the clucking of chickens.

But Keely?

When he looked at her, with her wild curls and her bright eyes, he saw a woman who already seemed a part of this land he loved.

Was he foolish to hope it was true?

Chapter Twelve

The sun hung low in the western sky, casting long shadows over the rolling pastures as William galloped toward the southern section of Eden's Gate. Jake and Logan flanked him, their horses keeping pace, the foreman's jaw tight with concern.

Just a short while earlier, Logan had ridden in with a troubling report. Cattle near the watering hole were showing signs of illness.

William's thoughts churned. He'd been in that exact area earlier in the day. Hadn't noticed a single sick cow. But then again, he hadn't been paying close attention to the herd after he spotted Keely out walking.

It had been nearly a month since Jake and one of the younger hands found a dead cow and her calf near the fence that bordered the Sanders ranch. Were these things connected? He didn't want to think so. Not if there'd been a chance to prevent it.

The three riders crested a rise. Below them, the

watering hole shimmered in the fading light, a cluster of cattle not far off. The animals stood awkwardly, tails switching, hooves striking at their own bellies. Some let out soft, distressed sounds. Others appeared dull and slow, their heads drooping.

Rocky and Tom were already there, keeping watch.

William reined in. "How many are sick?"

"A couple dozen, maybe," Rocky answered. "These here are scouring bad. Haven't seen it in the main herd yet. But I reckon we oughta move the rest north. Keep 'em clear of this water, just in case it's the cause."

William frowned. "We've never had trouble with this hole before. There's usually enough fresh water flowing through, especially in spring."

Jake nodded but added, "Still, Rocky's right. Better safe than sorry. We don't want to risk more catching whatever this is."

William's gaze returned to the listless cattle. "Think we'll lose any?"

"Hard to say," Jake said. "But I got a feelin' in my bones that they'll pull through."

"I hope your bones are right."

Jake gave a grunt in reply.

William exhaled slowly. "Looks like we're in for a long night." He turned Skunk toward the distant herd. "Logan, you'd better ride down to the Sanders' ranch and let Timothy know what's happened here. If there's trouble with the water farther up, it could affect his cattle too. Then go back to the house and let Mrs. Adler know we won't be back for dinner. Tell Chuck to throw together whatever he can and have you bring it back out."

"On it." Logan wheeled his horse around and galloped off.

William looked back at Rocky. "Keep watch on this bunch. If any try for a drink, drive 'em to the creek above the hole. Just to be safe."

Rocky gave a sharp nod. "Got it."

William shifted his reins. "All right, Jake, Tom. Let's move the main herd."

With that, he spurred Skunk forward, the thudding of hooves filling the space between worry and resolve. Tonight would be long, and maybe longer still if the sickness spread. But Eden's Gate had weathered worse. With God's help.

After Logan Coe left the house with a burlap sack full of sandwiches Chuck had packed for the men, Keely and Mrs. Adler ate their dinner in silence. From the looks exchanged between the cook and the housekeeper, Keely knew something was wrong, even if she didn't understand exactly what. Tension hung in the kitchen like smoke from a fire.

She was quietly grateful when Mrs. Adler stood, gathered her plate, and moved to the sink.

"I'm going to turn down Mr. William's bed," the housekeeper said, "so it'll be ready for him whenever he manages to get back." And with that, she left the kitchen.

Keely rose too. "Would you be wanting me to wash these dishes, Mr. Kincaid?"

Chuck shook his head. "No thanks. I've got it."

"'Twas very good, so it was."

"Appreciate you sayin' so."

She motioned toward the dining-room door. "There's just a few things I've to do before I turn in. Then I'll be off to bed meself. So I'll wish you goodnight now."

"Goodnight, Keely."

She moved toward the door, but his voice stopped her.

"Just so you know, if the men are out late, they won't go into Gibeon tomorrow for church. On Sundays like that, Mr. William usually holds a small service in the parlor for the boys who want to join him. You'll be welcome too."

"Thank you," she whispered, then stepped through the door and into the dining room.

In the parlor, she paused. Overhead, she heard the muffled thud of footsteps. Mrs. Adler moving about upstairs. Her heart quickened as she slipped quietly down the back hallway, her path lit only by the fading glow of twilight filtering in through the windows.

William's study was empty and shadowed, the corners blurred in dusk. The pale light of the dying day reached across the room just enough to guide her to the mantel. It was all she needed.

From the pocket of her apron, she drew the smooth stone. Her fingers curled around it instinctively. She rubbed it between thumb and forefinger, feeling again the calm weight of it. Would it be so wrong to keep it? Just for a little while longer?

In her mind's eye, she saw William's face. Not stern, not unreadable as he often was, but soft, and warm with that slight smile that barely touched the corners of his mouth. No, it would be wrong to keep it. It wasn't hers. 'Twas true the stone had no value in coins or dollars, but he'd kept it for a reason. One she didn't know but one that clearly mattered to him.

She stepped to the hearth and placed the stone gently beside the small wooden horse.

There. It was back where it belonged. But the strange thing was. It didn't make her feel better. Not in the least.

Upstairs, a floorboard creaked, and the sound spurred her into motion. She turned on her heel and slipped from the room, careful not to let the door make a sound as she closed it.

Outside, the gloaming lay thick over the barnyard, bathing the world in soft gray shadows. From around the corner, Rowdy appeared, silent as a shadow, tail wagging. He trotted to her side and bumped her hand with his nose. They'd become fast friends, the two of them, and she was thankful for his presence now. Tonight Rowdy's ears couldn't decide whether to stand straight or flop over, giving him a lopsided look that made her smile. But it was his eyes that undid her. Clear and trusting, full of mischief and devotion both, as if he understood every word she'd ever spoken.

"Come on, then," she said.

Rowdy swished his tail in answer.

He wasn't yet steady at his work, too eager to chase rather than guide. But she'd seen how he followed William's voice and hand, quick to learn, quick to please. And when she was alone, he was company for her, curling against her skirts as if he'd chosen her for his own.

At the cottage door, he nudged her hand again, eyes pleading.

She laughed under her breath and held a finger to her lips. "All right. In with you then. But mind you stay quiet. Mrs. Adler would not be pleased, and neither would William. And that's the truth."

He slipped through the doorway ahead of her, nails clicking softly on the wooden floor, already at home where he shouldn't be.

Perhaps a little like her own self.

The next morning, William came down the stairs before dawn, despite having spent only a few hours in his bed. And those few hours had been restless. His thoughts had churned all night, refusing to calm.

Two dozen cattle had sickened. But why?

Runoff from the mountains constantly fed that watering hole, keeping it cold, fresh, and always moving. He'd ridden by it just yesterday morning. The water had looked clear as ever. A man could see straight to the bottom without even squinting. Jake, Rocky, or any of the others would've noticed if something seemed off. A dead critter, a sheen on the surface, a foul smell. But no one had said a word about any of that.

Still, something had made those cattle sick. Discomfort and scouring didn't come out of nowhere.

If not the water, what then?

In the kitchen, he poured a large cup of coffee—God bless whoever had brewed it this morning—and carried it through the still-darkened house into his study. After lighting the lamp, he dropped into the chair behind his desk, the steam from the mug curling into the air like a question mark.

He considered pulling this year's ledger down from the shelf. Maybe scan for patterns in grazing rotation or water usage. But that would only give his worry more room to grow. Worry was a fire that didn't need more fuel.

Instead, he sat back and took a long sip of coffee, letting the quiet fall around him.

A gentle nudge stirred within his spirit. One he'd felt many times before. Scripture didn't command him to unravel every mystery on his own. It didn't tell him to carry his burdens until he broke beneath them. No, it said: Be anxious for nothing. Ask. Trust.

Trials would come. Of that he was sure. But he wasn't supposed to meet them with fear.

He closed his eyes and bowed his head.

"Father, there's a reason those cattle fell sick. I don't know what it is, but You do. The book of James says if I need wisdom, all I have to do is ask and believe You'll answer. So I'm asking. Open my eyes to see what You want to show me. Open my ears to hear when You speak."

He exhaled slowly and leaned back in his chair. It gave its usual groan of protest. A sound so familiar he didn't usually notice it. Except this morning, he did. It made him smile faintly, despite everything.

That's when his eyes drifted toward the mantel. And he stilled. Was that—?

He rose, coffee forgotten, and stepped across the room. Reaching out, he picked up the smooth stone resting beside the small wooden horse. His fingers closed around it.

It was back.

For nearly a month, it had been gone. He hadn't spoken about it. Not to Mrs. Adler, not to Keely, not to anyone. Why would he? He'd only noticed its absence when he was here, in this room, alone with his thoughts. Then, the moment he left the study, more pressing matters always pushed it from his mind.

But now it was back. He didn't know where it had been or how it had found its way back. None of that mattered to him at the moment.

The familiar weight of the stone settled into his palm. A boyhood treasure. A token of a simpler time. Of skipping stones with his mother and laughing until their sides ached. That small stone had no value to anyone else. But to him, it was something precious.

He swallowed hard.

"You feed the sparrows," he whispered, voice thick. "You clothe the lilies of the field." His fingers tightened gently around the stone. "You even care that I misplaced this." Eyes closed, he let the moment linger before adding, "Thank You for returning it."

After a few more breaths, he slipped the stone back into its place on the mantel and turned toward the door. Whatever this day would bring, he felt more ready to face it now than he had just minutes before.

Chapter Thirteen

As predicted, no one from Eden's Gate rode into Gibeon that Sunday morning for church. Instead, those who wished gathered in the parlor of the main house for a time of Scripture reading and prayer. Keely joined the small congregation, seated beside Mrs. Adler on the sofa, while Jake and Logan settled into a pair of straight-backed chairs behind the sofa. William took one wingback near the hearth, his Bible already open on his lap.

When the room grew quiet, he began to read: "'If any of you lack wisdom, let him ask of God, that giveth to all men liberally, and upbraideth not; and it shall be given him. But let him ask in faith, nothing wavering. For he that wavereth is like a wave of the sea driven with the wind and tossed.'"

He lifted his gaze from the well-worn pages, voice steady. "When I woke this morning, I felt anxious. Couldn't stop thinking about the cattle. Wondering what caused the sickness. But then I remembered God's command not to worry. Worrying doesn't add a single hour to my life. Might even take a few away. So instead, I asked Him for wisdom. The Bible promises He'll give it if I ask, and I'm trusting that He will. I'm hoping the rest of you will do the same."

Keely felt something stir in her chest.

William wasn't just reciting words. He believed them. Every syllable. She could see it in the way he spoke, in the quiet conviction behind each sentence. He believed the Bible held the answers to life. And he lived as if it mattered.

How had he come to believe so deeply?

Her mam had believed like that too. Trusted, even when there'd been no earthly reason to. But what good had it done? Her da had sickened and died despite all of Mam's prayers. Then Mam herself had gone. And Keely? She had to fend for herself any way she could.

She heard her mother's voice again, an echo from the past: *"He knows the number of my days, Keely girl. He won't be taking me home too early or too late. And He has yourself in the palm of His hand, too. You can trust Him with the future, even when I'm not with you."*

Was that true? Did God hold her in His palm? She believed He was there, watching. She even believed Jesus came to die for her sins, which were legion. Or so it seemed. But was He wanting to guide her steps, to take away her worry, to give her wisdom?

She tried to return her focus to the present. William was reading again, but the words sounded far away. She watched as he closed the Bible and said simply, "Let's pray."

To her left, Mrs. Adler bowed her head and closed her eyes. Keely assumed Jake and Logan had done the same behind her. She followed suit, lowering her head as William began to pray the Lord's Prayer aloud. A prayer she had learned at her mam's knees.

But her heart was shouting a question she couldn't silence: *Do You care for me, God, as Mam said You did? Even when I'm doin' the things I shouldn't?*

"'Thy kingdom come,'" William's voice rang out, calm and reverent, "'Thy will be done in earth, as it is in heaven.'"

Tears welled up unbidden. *I want to trust You, Father. The way Mam did. The way William does. Help me, please.*

"'For thine is the kingdom, and the power, and the glory, forever. Amen.'"

"Amen," she whispered. She wasn't sure if the word was her response to the end of the Lord's Prayer or to her own private, silent plea.

She dabbed at her eyes with a handkerchief, and when she looked up, William's gaze met hers. He wore a quiet smile, gentle and unassuming.

He thinks me better than I am. She swallowed hard and looked away, ashamed. *And I'm far worse than he can ever know. Liar. Thief. And not anything I should be.*

She rose abruptly. "I'm sorry," she murmured, and left the parlor without waiting for a response. She hurried out the front door and didn't stop until she reached the corral fence. Her hands wrapped tightly around the top rail as her pulse hammered in her throat.

She couldn't seem to breathe right. As if the sky itself couldn't offer enough air.

And then the tears came again, hot and fast.

"Miss Boyle?"

She stiffened, gripping the rail even tighter, not turning to face him.

"Are you all right?" William's voice was closer now. He stepped up to the fence but kept his distance.

"Yes." The word scraped out of her throat, more croak than whisper.

He said nothing more, but she sensed he was waiting. Giving her space, giving her time. She didn't know if that made her want to sob harder or fling something at him for being so blasted patient.

She wiped her tears away with the back of her hand, realizing her handkerchief was gone, lost somewhere between the parlor and here.

"I believe you could use this." His voice was soft, and when she turned slightly, she saw him holding out a kerchief of his own.

She took it without meeting his eyes. "Thank you kindly."

"Whatever troubles you, Miss Boyle, God can handle it."

She almost laughed at that—only it wasn't funny.

Sure and it must be easy for someone like him to believe God would make a way. His mother had left him this ranch, all this land and the cattle on it. He hadn't been left in poverty as she had, forced to scrape for whatever he had. Oh, he worked hard. She'd witnessed that for herself. But it was easier to trust in a God who saw to it that one didn't go hungry. Harder when one went without.

She heard her mam's voice again: *"The Lord is my shepherd; I shall not want."*

Her gut twisted. Bitterness surged. "But I have been in want," she muttered under her breath.

"What was that?"

She turned toward him, and all the helpless, knotted-up ache inside her tangled with fury. Not just at God but at *him*, too. At William Overstreet, with his warm smile, his calm certainty, and his eyes that saw her better than she saw herself.

Sweet sufferin' cats!

She was angry enough to hit him. Just for being good. Just for being kind.

Just for being himself.

William watched Keely whirl away, skirts lifted high to keep from tripping in her haste. Rowdy appeared out of nowhere, loping after her like a loyal shadow, disappearing with her into the cottage.

What had he said? What had he done?

She'd suddenly been burning with anger. He'd seen it flash in her eyes. Those green eyes that had brimmed not long before with tears. Then they'd sparked like flint.

He played the scene back in his mind. She'd been tearful, moved by something in the worship service, he'd thought. She'd gone outside. He'd followed her, offering her his kerchief when she'd clearly lost her own. She'd thanked him. He'd tried to reassure her that God could handle whatever burden she was carrying. Then she'd muttered something he hadn't caught. And just like that, she'd turned on him.

The anger had come off her in waves. He could've sworn he felt the heat of it.

He ran his fingers through his hair, frustrated. For the life of him, he couldn't make sense of it. True, he had little experience with women. His school years had been spent surrounded by other boys, and most of his adult life had unfolded right here on Eden's Gate, elbow-deep in work and surrounded by cowhands.

He mentally walked through the exchange again, searching for missteps. Nothing. Still no clue.

Fortunately, a distraction arrived in the form of Mick Chandler. The seasoned cowboy rode in from the south, dust trailing behind him. He was older than most of the other men—only Jake had more years—and had been hired on just before calving season in late February.

Mick reined in his horse and tipped his hat back. "Rocky wanted you to know that none of the cows died overnight. They're looking better this morning. Not in near as much distress."

William exhaled a breath he hadn't realized he was holding. "That's good to hear." He stepped back from the corral fence. "Have you eaten?"

"Nope."

"Then grab yourself some grub and get some rest. I'll ride out in a while and spell Rocky."

"You got it, boss." Mick tipped his hat again and turned his horse toward the hitching post.

William glanced once more toward the guest cottage, then headed for the main house.

The parlor stood empty, the morning gathering now a memory. The straight-backed chairs had been returned to their places around the dining table. He figured Jake and Logan had slipped off to the bunkhouse. Mrs. Adler was likely in her own quarters, and Chuck was either resting or prepping the next meal. Honestly, William had never figured out when the cook slept.

Well, no use pondering it now. He needed to head back out. No time for dawdling.

He took the stairs two at a time. In his room, he exchanged his Sunday clothes for work gear, then made his way back downstairs. Passing through the kitchen, he paused just long enough to tell Chuck what he needed.

"Lunch to go," he said. "Whatever's easy to pack."

"I'll fix something."

William nodded his thanks and headed to the barn.

From his stall, Skunk nickered and tossed his head, eager for a run. William gave him a fond pat on the neck. "Not today, boy. Sage needs the miles."

The stallion huffed in protest, stomping a hoof as if offended by the demotion.

William laughed under his breath. "You'll live."

He walked on to the last stall, where the young mare waited, ears forward, eyes alert. She was still learning but steady. And she could cover ground with smooth efficiency.

Less than half an hour later, with lunch tucked in the

saddlebag, William rode Sage out of the barnyard. The sun was warm on his face, the morning breeze mild. Spring was holding strong, but the coming heat of summer wasn't far off. Maybe a month. Maybe less.

As he rode, his eyes scanned the land with the practiced ease of a man who knew every dip and rise by heart. The grass was green, a comfort after the previous year's drought. Pale shoots waved near the crests. Down in the draws, where moisture lingered, the blue-green blades grew thick and lush.

It was the kind of spring that gave a rancher hope. Hope for strong calves, fattening herds, and a profitable season. But William's mind wasn't at ease. He couldn't shake the image of those cattle, staggering and dull-eyed. Scouring didn't happen without a reason. Something had set them off.

The grass? Too rich, maybe. But not for the cows. Calves, sure, might bloat on it, but not the cows.

That left the water. But what was wrong with it? He needed answers. God help him, he hoped he got them soon.

In a strange way, he realized, he was glad for the plaguing thoughts and troublesome questions. They kept his mind from returning once again to the angry Irish miss he'd left behind him at the ranch house.

Chapter Fourteen

With a scrub brush in her right hand and a dripping rag in the left, Keely bent low, her weight balanced on aching knees as she worked the soap into the wide pine planks of the kitchen floor. The suds darkened with every stroke, proof that even a fine ranch house like Eden's Gate gathered its share of dirt. The wood, worn pale from years of scouring, was smooth beneath her fingers, though the knots and stubborn grain reminded her that no matter how hard she scrubbed, perfection would never come.

She pressed harder, muscles burning. The ache in her arms was welcome, a distraction from the heavier ache lodged in her chest. Better to feel strain in her limbs than to dwell on the storm inside her.

Two days had passed since she'd marched away from William in a rage. Two days of letting that fury simmer and steep. Thankfully, they'd not crossed paths again. Good. Let him stay busy with his cattle and his fences and his ranch hands. She wanted nothing to do with that calm strength, or the way his eyes seemed to look right through her when he spoke.

Every time she thought about the easy road his life seemed to follow—born into land, legacy, and leadership—her jaw clenched. She'd fought for every crust of bread. Worked her fingers raw for others and still ended up on her knees, scrubbing floors. Why had God favored him and not her? Her conscience always twinged when that question passed through her head. After all, why would God favor a thief? But she wouldn't have stolen anything if she hadn't been in need.

The sharp sting of lye rose around her, biting her nose. But no matter how strong the soap, it couldn't scour away the bitterness she felt.

Her mam would've had something to say about that. Mam always did. Bitterness, she'd warned, only made sorrow deepen. *"Sure and it won't help you, Keely girl. It'll keep you down."*

"I don't want to feel this way," she muttered in response. "Don't want to, but I do."

She shifted to the next board and set to scrubbing again. That's when the back door slammed open, bringing a gust of air and Chuck with it, a sack of potatoes slung over his shoulder.

"Good morning, Keely." He stomped his boots on the threshold and reached back to close the door, only to be thwarted by a blur of brown and white fur.

"Rowdy, no!" Keely dropped the brush and reached for the pup, but he dodged her grasp. His paw clipped the edge of the bucket, and with a mighty splash, soapy water flooded across the freshly scrubbed floor.

Keely gasped as water fanned in all directions. Suds splattered her skirt and soaked her knees. Rowdy, delighted by the chaos, skidded through the puddle, tail waving, paws slipping this way and that.

Chuck barked out a laugh. "Looks like the pup wants to help you clean. Better tie a brush to his tail and let him go."

Keely's lips twitched against her will. "A help like that, I'll not be done 'til Christmas." She lunged for Rowdy again, but he darted behind Chuck's legs and gave a vigorous shake, spraying both of them in a fine mist.

The cook roared with amusement, setting the potatoes down before he toppled over with mirth. "I declare, you'll not get peace so long as that scallywag is at your side."

She clutched her dripping wash rag and laughed too, her earlier bitterness forgotten.

At that moment the dining-room door swung open, and Mrs. Adler stepped in. Her sharp gaze swept the kitchen, taking in the puddles, the paw prints, and the dog. Her gasp echoed to the rafters. "Get that filthy mutt out of my kitchen!"

Rowdy froze, ears down, as if even he knew he'd gone too far.

"He could be crawling with vermin for all we know!" Mrs. Adler flapped her apron toward him.

Chuck moved quickly to open the door. Sensing the urgency, Rowdy bolted through it without protest.

Trying to hide her smile, Keely said, "He's not crawling with vermin, Mrs. Adler. I promise you that."

The woman planted her fists on her hips. "You've made a pet of him, I suppose."

"I'm thinkin' I don't know your meaning." Keely bent to mop up the soapy mess.

"You most certainly do. I've seen how you are with that dog. You'll spoil him, and that won't do Mr. William any favors."

"Leave the girl alone," Chuck said, his voice calm but firm. "I'm the one who let the pup in. It wasn't her fault."

The housekeeper gave a huff and turned on her heel, disappearing back into the dining room with a mutter and a shake of her head.

Keely glanced over her shoulder. "Thank you kindly, Mr. Kincaid."

Chuck chuckled, wiping a hand down his apron. "This kitchen's seen worse than a pup with wet feet. Dug a bullet outta a man's leg on that very table once. Blood everywhere. Now that was a mess."

"I'll be believing that."

He grinned. "Don't mind Mrs. Adler too much. She barks loud, but her bite's mostly for show."

Keely nodded, her heart softening again. Yes, there were kindnesses here. Far more than she'd expected and certainly more than she deserved.

She got back down on her knees to wipe up the rest of the water, the brush forgotten for now. And while she was there, she whispered a prayer—quiet, unsure— asking God, if He was still listening to the likes of her, to take the bitter root out of her heart.

The way her mam would've wanted.

William returned to the house mid-afternoon. Though he preferred being out on the range in this beautiful spring weather, he could delay the papers waiting on his desk no longer.

He settled into the chair in his study, the familiar scent of ink and old leather thick in the small room. Ledger books lay open before him, their tidy columns awaiting his attention. He ran a hand over his jaw, wishing the numbers would add themselves. Figures had never come easily to him. Cattle, horses, land—those he understood. Jocelyn had always been the one with a sharp mind for sums and details.

Still, he forced himself to reckon the accounts, scratching notes with a blunt pencil. Beside the ledger lay a letter from the Teton Stock Growers' Association, urging attendance at next week's meeting in Blackfoot. He'd planned to go regardless, but the recent sickness among his cattle lent the trip new urgency. If other ranchers had dealt with similar troubles, he wanted to know—and face to face.

A knock interrupted his thoughts.

"Come in," he called.

The door eased open, and Keely stepped in, balancing a tray with a steaming coffeepot and a single mug. "Mrs. Adler thought you might be wanting some coffee."

He leaned back with a weary smile. "Tell her I thank her. And you as well."

She set the tray on the corner of his desk, then hesitated, her eyes flicking to the ledger, then to the letter with its bold heading. "I'm thinking you work very hard to keep what you have."

He shrugged lightly. "Ranching isn't easy. Not often. But I love it."

"I was wrong to think it came easy to you." A flush rose in her cheeks.

He remembered the way she'd stalked off two days ago, obviously angry with him without him knowing why. She wasn't angry now. She seemed almost . . . repentant. There was more behind her words than he understood. Of that, he was certain.

"Sir?" She glanced up at him. "I overheard Mr. Kincaid talking with Logan Coe earlier. About the sick cattle. I knew of the trouble, but I wasn't understanding it all until now."

"What do you mean?"

"What I might have seen." Her hands tightened in front of her apron. "The day before the cows took sick, the day you found me by the creek and walked back with me." She hesitated.

He nodded. "Go on."

"I saw a man ride up to the watering hole. I wasn't near enough to say who he was, only that it wasn't you." She paused, the color deepening on her face. "I'd recognize your horse and your seat. This wasn't you."

"No," he said gently. "It wasn't."

"He got down, went to the water's edge. Maybe he just wanted a drink. I wouldn't be knowing. He knelt there for a bit, then mounted up and rode off, heading south. I thought nothing of it at the time. But now . . . if that's where the cows sickened . . . maybe he didn't belong there." Her voice trailed off, uncertain.

William's jaw clenched. He'd considered every natural cause—bad grass, stagnant water, dead animal, sickness carried in—but this was something else. A man who might not belong on Eden's Gate opened up darker possibilities.

"You did right to tell me, Miss Boyle," he said at last, keeping his voice calm though his mind spun. "Thank you."

She dipped him the smallest of curtsies—something she rarely did anymore, and he was glad of it—before turning and leaving the study.

William sat still for a long moment, staring at the grain of the wooden desktop without really seeing it.

In this country, a man's herd was his livelihood, his standing, his very survival. Had someone sought to do him harm? And why would they?

To weaken a neighbor's cattle could mean driving him into debt. Or driving him out altogether. It might be spite, born of a grudge carried too long. It might be greed, with one rancher hoping to enlarge his holdings by forcing another to sell cheap. Or it might be the simple meanness of a man who couldn't abide competition.

He blew out a breath and shoved the cooling coffee aside.

This land was more than his living. It was his legacy. His grandfather's sweat, his mother's devotion, his own hard years building Eden's Gate into something worth passing on. He would not see it undone through the secret dealings of cowards.

His gaze shifted to the stock growers' letter. The meeting in Blackfoot couldn't come soon enough. If other ranchers had seen signs of trouble—unexplained sickness, strangers near their boundaries—he needed to hear it firsthand. And if this problem was his alone, then he'd better find out fast how to handle it before it happened again.

Until then, he would keep his men alert. And his eyes sharper still.

The cattle were recovering, thank God, but he would not rest easy. Not while questions lingered at the bottom of a watering hole.

Chapter Fifteen

Roger and Victoria came to Eden's Gate after church the following Sunday. After William and the Bernhardts finished their midday meal, Victoria pushed back from the table with a dramatic sigh. "I am so full I'm miserable. I'll sit on the porch and stare at the mountains while I recover."

"Are you all right?" Roger asked softly. "Would you like me to join you?"

"I am perfectly all right, darling. You stay and talk with William. I'll be quite content on my own."

With a nod, Roger settled back into his chair.

Wondering if his friend was concerned, William leaned toward him. "Is she *truly* all right?"

"She would have said if she wasn't. Honestly, she's doing very well. No more daily naps. To be truthful, I think she has more energy than I do. But the other mothers in town keep warning her to sleep all she can now, before the baby comes and sleep becomes a luxury."

William chuckled. "Sound advice, I imagine." He stood. "Shall we retire to the study?"

"If you wish."

"There's something I'd like to talk over with you." William led the way from the dining room, then paused. "Would you like me to ask Mrs. Adler to bring some tea?"

"Thank you, no. I daresay I'm as full as Victoria."

Both men laughed as they stepped into the study. There was no fire on the hearth, and the shaded room remained pleasantly cool, even with the afternoon sun streaming through the window.

William claimed his usual chair near the fireplace.

Roger sat opposite him. "What is bothering you, my friend?"

William didn't hesitate. He laid out everything about the sick cattle, the watering hole, and Keely's report of the man she'd seen kneeling near the water. "I've checked with all the boys," he added. "None of them recall being down there that day. They were working the herd to the north."

Roger's brow furrowed. "So you suspect foul play?"

"I don't know," he admitted as he rubbed the back of his neck. "But I can't believe it was something natural. Not with the way it happened. I'm heading to Blackfoot this week for the stock growers' meeting. Maybe someone else has seen similar trouble."

"By Jove! Blackfoot?" Roger's expression brightened. "I need to meet with a solicitor there. The man's contacted me twice already, but I keep putting it off."

"A lawyer? Is something amiss?"

"Nothing serious. Just lingering business with my father's estate. Tedious matters."

"I didn't know that had dragged on this long."

"My sentiments exactly," Roger said. "Still, I need to settle it. Would you mind terribly if I came along?"

"Not at all. I'd be glad for your company."

Roger hesitated. "I should mention . . . I believe Victoria will want to come too."

William had planned to ride out with Jake, traveling light and fast. But if Victoria joined them, they would need the surrey. They couldn't expect a mother-to-be to travel on horseback. The light wagon meant a slower pace, turning a two-day ride into three. They'd have to stop in Rexburg and Idaho Falls for the nights. No camping under the stars. But if he were being honest, the idea of a warm bed didn't sound so bad. Nights in May could still be bitterly cold.

Roger seemed to sense his conflict. "If that's an inconvenience—" he began.

William held up a hand. "Not at all. I wasn't hesitating because I objected. Just making plans in my head. I'd be glad to have you both along." He paused. "We'll need to leave Tuesday morning. Will that work?"

"Perfectly. That's jolly good." Then, sitting back in his chair, Roger said, "Now didn't you mention something else you wished to discuss with me?"

Keely stepped out of the cottage, Rowdy close on her heels. In the five days since the mishap in the kitchen, the young canine had become more determined than ever to claim her as his own. And truth be told, Keely didn't have it in her heart to discourage him, no matter what Mrs. Adler might say. She'd never had a pet before. Never had anything much to call her own, really. And it was more than lovely to be looked at with such open devotion. Even if the one doing the looking was a gangly creature with too much energy and not enough sense.

"Keely! Hello!"

She turned toward the porch and saw Victoria seated in the shade, her hands resting lightly on the gentle curve of her belly, her pregnancy only now becoming obvious to everyone.

"Come and join me."

Even now, more than a month into her time at Eden's Gate, Keely still felt a quiet surprise whenever someone like Victoria Bernhardt treated her as an equal. It was unexpected, uncomfortable . . . and oddly warming.

"Please," Victoria added with a smile.

With a nod, she complied.

"And who's this with you?"

Keely glanced down. "This is Rowdy. Sure and the name suits him."

"Roger and I have a cat. Her name is Hope." Victoria motioned to the chair beside her. "Sit with me, won't you?"

Keely took the few steps up to the porch and moved toward the indicated chair, certain that Mrs. Adler wouldn't approve. Wasn't this a little like letting a filthy dog into the kitchen? She imagined herself slopping wash water onto Victoria's skirts and cringed.

"We haven't really visited since that afternoon at Miss Irene's," Victoria said, folding her hands again over her belly, a protective sort of gesture. "Gracious, that was weeks ago now. How have you been?"

"I'm well, thank you." Keely felt her cheeks warm. She never knew what to say when people asked about her, especially in such a friendly way. "And yourself?"

"Oh, I'm well. Exceedingly so." There was a brightness in Victoria's eyes, a peaceful glow. "You know, Keely, I'm fairly new to Gibeon too. I didn't come from across the sea, but I came a long way. As a girl, I used to walk along the Atlantic shore. I imagine you did the same on your side of the ocean."

Keely swallowed hard. When would she have had time to walk by the sea? But she didn't say it.

"Since we're both newcomers," Victoria went on, "I think we should become friends. Don't you?"

Keely's eyes widened.

Victoria looked as though she might say more, but just then the front door opened. Roger stepped outside, followed closely by William.

"I have news," Roger said, his voice bright. "We're going to Blackfoot. William has business there with the stock growers' association, and I need to meet with Mr. Henry and take care of that legal matter I mentioned. So, you and I are going to accompany him and Jake Foster. We'll leave on Tuesday. Is this enough notice for you to be ready?"

"One day should be plenty. How long will we be gone?"

"A little over a week."

Keely shifted in her seat, wishing she could rise and slip away unnoticed. But the two men blocked the steps, and while Roger's gaze remained fixed on his wife, Keely could feel William looking at her. She didn't turn her head to check. She didn't need to.

"Keely should come with us," Victoria said suddenly, her voice firm with conviction.

It took a moment for the words to register. "Me? Why would I be going with you?"

"To keep me company, of course," the other woman said with a laugh. "I'd rather not be the only female on the trip. And besides, it'll give us a chance to know each other better."

"I'm thinking Mrs. Adler wouldn't be liking the idea—"

"I daresay," Roger interrupted, "Mrs. Adler can do without you for a week or so."

"But I—"

"It's all right." William's voice was full of quiet authority that brooked no further argument. "It won't be any hardship for Mrs. Adler. With me gone there won't be as much to do anyway. I'll inform her of why you'll be absent from the house."

Rowdy whimpered and placed a paw on Keely's knee, as if in protest.

"And that scamp," William added with a chuckle, "will have to fend for himself until you get back."

Chapter Sixteen

K eely and the small party set off early Tuesday morning, long before the sun crested the jagged peaks of the Tetons. The world still wore its twilight hush, the sky streaked with the faintest blush of dawn.

William and Jake rode on horseback, leading the way. Roger drove the team with ease, his hands sure on the reins. Both women—Victoria seated beside her husband, and Keely tucked into the rear seat—had blankets wrapped around their laps to guard against the lingering chill of spring.

The ranch had slipped from view some time ago, its fences and pastures lost behind them, when Victoria turned slightly and said, "Keely, did you know Roger and I met while traveling? In fact, I would venture to say a good part of our courtship took place in a coach. Wouldn't you agree, dearest?"

Roger chuckled. "It does seem that way."

Keely smiled, but something inside her cinched tight.

She didn't carry the same feelings for Roger that she once had. She'd let go of that foolish infatuation. But watching the quiet glances pass between him and Victoria—the shared warmth, the gentle touch of her hand to his sleeve—those things stirred a longing deep within her chest. Was it so wrong to wish for that kind of love? That kind of belonging?

Her eyes drifted forward without meaning to, to where William rode astride a tall palomino gelding. The morning light cast him in sharp silhouette—broad shoulders, straight spine, easy grip on the reins, confident and quiet, commanding without trying. A woman would be safe with him.

But he isn't for the likes o' me.

She drew a slow breath and forced herself to look away. Best not to think such thoughts. They'd only lead to heartache. Instead, she fixed her attention on the conversation at hand as Victoria recounted how she and Roger had first met on a road in Yellowstone, she in search of her half-brother. Roger picked up the tale with a smile, adding details Keely hadn't heard before. They shared the story like one might pass a cherished quilt between them, each laying a hand on a corner, smoothing it with affection.

Every time Victoria touched his arm, Roger turned toward her with a look so full of adoration it made Keely's throat tighten.

How could anyone not envy such tenderness?

A couple of hours passed before they stopped to rest the horses and stretch their legs. Victoria leaned close to her husband and whispered a need, and Roger, ever gallant, walked with her to a nearby stand of trees, where he stood guard while she vanished behind a screen of green.

Keely took her chance to stretch her legs too, wandering a short distance in the opposite direction. She didn't realize she was being followed until William's voice called gently behind her.

"Don't wander too far, Miss Boyle."

She turned to find him just a few paces away.

"You need to watch where you step. The rattlers'll be out of their dens by now. They like rocky slopes and sunny patches." His eyes scanned the area, calm but alert. "Like this one."

She swallowed, her skin prickling. "I'll mind where I walk, so I will." Mrs. Adler had warned her about the venomous snakes, though Keely had yet to see one herself. And if she had her way, she never would. She loathed anything that slithered.

On the next part of the journey, Jake traded places with Roger, and Victoria moved to the back to sit beside Keely. After a lengthy but comfortable silence, she released a sigh. "I must say that being married to an artist has made me much more aware of the world around me. Idaho is so beautiful."

"Aye, it is."

"And you said you loved to watch Roger paint when you were both in England. I know exactly what you mean. I love watching him when he's working, too."

"It wasn't often I had that pleasure, to see him painting, though he always made me welcome when I'd come across him. Sure and I don't know how he puts what he sees in his mind onto paper. His watercolors of Hooke Manor were so beautiful." She touched her breastbone with the fingers of one hand. "But the oil painting that he sent to his lordship? It took my breath away."

"I know exactly what you mean, Keely. I feel the same. Although now I'm a little envious that you have seen Hooke Manor and I have not. For it is such a large part of Roger's past."

Keely drew back slightly. "You're envious of me?"

"Why wouldn't I be?" Victoria smiled again, gently. "You're so full of life, and you have such courage."

She blinked. Full of life? Courage? The words sounded strange to her. No one had ever said such things about her before. She wasn't brave. She was surviving. That was all.

Her thoughts drifted, unbidden, to the smooth skipping stone she'd taken from William's mantel. For days she'd kept it tucked beside a brooch in a drawer by her bed. Occasionally, she'd lifted it out just to feel it in her hand. In those moments, it had felt like hers. Not the stone, really, but perhaps the memory it carried. Or maybe the person it belonged to. But it hadn't been hers to keep, and it never would be. That was why she'd returned it to its place. Quietly. Without a word.

She looked down at her hands. No, no one had any reason to envy her.

As if sensing the turn of her thoughts, Victoria reached out and laid her hand over Keely's. Warm and gentle, the gesture said what words didn't need to. Keely met her eyes, and for a long moment, neither woman spoke. They simply sat with the sound of the wagon wheels turning, the creak of leather, and the hush of wind in the grass.

Seated on Goldrush, William led the small party into the small town of Rexburg, the sun hanging low in the west. He guided them toward the only boarding house the town offered. He'd stayed there before. Once. Maybe twice. Not by choice, but by necessity. If there had been another decent roof under which to shelter, he would have taken it.

Inside the boarding house, the air smelled of boiled cabbage, damp wool, and old varnish. The rooms were quickly assigned—one for the women and another for the three men—and they just managed to wash up before the supper bell rang.

The long oak table in the dining room groaned more under its age than under the weight of the meal. Chipped platters and bowls crowded the center, filled with offerings that looked more hopeful than hearty. A grayish stew, thick with turnips and overcooked potatoes, sent up a nose-stinging steam heavy with onions. A pan of biscuits sat beside it, pale and lopsided, their centers still slightly doughy where the heat hadn't reached.

"Best eat up while it's hot," said Mrs. Beardsley, the broad-shouldered proprietress, as she ladled stew into their bowls with a wide grin.

Across the table from William, a traveling salesman in a loud plaid coat was already half-finished with his stew, shoveling it in like it was the finest fare west of the Mississippi. He didn't so much as glance up when William bowed his head to give thanks. Jake, Roger, Keely, and Victoria followed suit, adding their quiet Amen to his prayer.

William lifted his spoon, braced himself, and took a bite. It tasted exactly as it looked—watery and underseasoned, the turnips too sharp, the potatoes too soft, and hardly a trace of beef to speak of. He forced the bite down and lowered his spoon again. Chuck's roast beef and gravy flashed across his memory. Then came the thought of the ranch cook's peach pie, flaky and warm, and he nearly groaned aloud.

At the far end of the table, Jake caught his eye and gave him a dry, knowing smirk. William allowed the corner of his mouth to twitch in response. They needed no words. Both were thinking the same thing: This wasn't anything like the dinner table at Eden's Gate. Not by half.

Judging by the expressions on the others' faces as they ate, everyone—except for that salesman—shared the same sentiment. Still, road hunger proved stronger than their sense of taste. Plates emptied, but the conversation never started. Whether from weariness or the unappetizing food, no one seemed inclined to linger.

His bowl close to empty, William stood and stretched, rubbing the back of his neck as he walked toward the stairs. Roger was already escorting the women down the hall to their room.

"If it's all right with you, boss," Jake said in a low

voice beside him, "I figured I'd check on the horses before I call it a night."

"Of course." William nodded, though his thoughts were elsewhere.

Outside the women's room, Roger had paused and gently tilted Victoria's face upward, brushing a kiss against her lips. Keely stood quietly behind them, her hands folded in front of her, gaze respectfully averted.

But William had seen the kiss. Seen how Roger lingered, how Victoria's fingers curled into his lapel. There was nothing improper about it. Only tenderness. A husband cherishing his wife. Still, something inside William shifted, not unlike how a saddle might slip if cinched too loosely. He looked away.

Lucky Roger.

Jake caught his eye again and gave a nod. "I won't be long enough for you to nod off, I reckon."

"Right." He cleared his throat.

Jake tugged on his hat and disappeared through the front door. William stood there a moment longer, rooted in place, watching the empty hallway. He couldn't say why the kiss had gotten under his skin the way it had. He wasn't the envious sort. At least, he'd never thought so. But the image lingered. And it wasn't Roger's face he kept seeing. It was his own. And it wasn't Victoria in that imagined moment either.

It was Keely.

He clenched his jaw and forced the thought away. Fool notion, he told himself. She worked for him. She was under his roof and his protection. That was all. She wasn't for him. Couldn't be. A man needed to know where the lines were.

He exhaled hard through his nose and started up the stairs, his boots thudding against the worn treads. The door to the men's room creaked as he opened it, and the lamplight glowed low inside. He didn't bother to undress, just sat on the edge of the bed and ran both hands over his face. Despite the ache in his limbs from the long ride, sleep felt far off.

Too many thoughts crowded close. Questions without answers. Feelings without welcome. Images of green eyes, red curls, and a heart too complicated for his keeping.

He reached over, turned down the lamp, and lay back.

It would be a long night.

Chapter Seventeen

Keely could not help but think of Mr. Kincaid's hearty flapjacks and golden-crusted loaves of bread when she sat down to the breakfast served in the Rexburg boarding house. The eggs lay pale and runny, leaking across her plate into curls of limp bacon that were more fat than meat. The toast was burnt black at the edges, the middle soft and soggy. When she reached for a slice, flakes of char stuck to her fingertips. The coffee bit the tongue and sat heavy in the stomach.

But a roof over one's head and food in one's belly, no matter how poorly prepared, weren't to be despised. She'd learned that much in the lean years, when even spoiled bread could seem a blessing if it kept the hunger away. So when she stepped through the boarding house doorway a short while later, shawl tugged close against the morning chill, she still smiled at Mrs. Beardsley and thanked her for her hospitality.

Outside, the surrey waited at the hitching post, already loaded. Victoria sat on the back bench, the folds of her traveling dress tucked neatly around her.

"Keely, you'll need to ride up front," she said, cheerful despite the hour. "I hope you don't mind. Roger insists on beginning the day at my side."

"Sure and that's being fine with me."

As Keely moved toward the buggy, her gaze fell on the palomino gelding tied behind it. The other saddle horse stood nearby, Jake Foster tightening the cinch.

Her pulse gave a sudden skip. She didn't need to guess what that meant.

William stepped up beside her. "Allow me," he said, offering his hand.

There was a brief pause before she took it. His fingers were rough from work, warm even in the morning cold. She climbed up onto the front bench and settled herself with as much composure as she could manage, draping the spare blanket across her lap.

William rounded the front of the team and mounted the seat beside her. "All right," he called to Jake as he gathered the reins. "Let's get moving." He slapped the leather against the horses' rumps, and with a jerk, they were off on another day of travel.

The surrey rattled down the street and out of town, the wheels clattering over ruts and hard-packed dirt. The morning sun reached long fingers across the flat, awakening the land with a wash of gold and pink. Keely tucked her hands beneath the blanket and sat still, all too aware of the man beside her.

Roger's voice soon carried forward from the seat behind them. "I confess, William, I find these wide spaces a challenge to my craft. In England, there is always a hedgerow, a church spire, a curve of lane to anchor the eye. Here, it is sky and more sky. Beautiful, yes, but daunting to put on canvas."

William let out a low chuckle, eyes steady on the road ahead. "Daunting or not, it's the truth of the land. Out here, a man doesn't want to be hemmed in. A spire might be pretty in a painting, but it won't water cattle or keep them fed come winter."

"True enough. Yet you must know what I mean. The sweep of the plain can almost swallow the eye. I long to capture that sense of immensity without losing the details that make it real. The bending of grass in the wind. The way the light shifts against the Tetons."

"That's a trick of your trade, I suppose," William said. "My work's simpler. A patch of grass might look green enough to you, but I look at it and see whether I've got three days of feed or five. How much weight the herd'll carry by season's end."

Roger gave a thoughtful grunt. "And yet we are both, in our own way, measuring the land."

Keely listened in silence, fascinated by the ease between them. So different, these two men, but neither dismissing the other. Roger's voice held poetry, a longing to create something lasting with brush and pigment. William's tone was practical, grounded, steady. But each understood the land in his own way. And both, she realized, loved it.

How strange, she thought, that the same earth can

speak to two men in such different tongues. And she wondered why she cared so very much about one of them.

She shifted slightly on the seat. The rhythm of the horses' hooves set a steady beat as her thoughts wandered to the evening before. She hadn't meant to spy on a private moment between husband and wife. But as she'd moved into the bedroom that she would share with Victoria, she looked back. That was when Roger bent to kiss his wife's upturned face a second time. Seeing it, Keely's breath caught in her throat. It was such a simple gesture. No more than the meeting of lips, tender and sure. But it carried a world of meaning. Love and belonging. Safety. A promise that a woman mattered enough to be cherished.

Keely had turned away quickly, but the image had followed her into her dreams. And so had another. One darker and harder to forget. Mr. Brown. His lips forced against hers. The smell of wine on his breath. The weight of his body pressed where it had no right to be. Her heart had pounded with fear, not yearning. His touch had burned, not warmed.

She closed her eyes briefly, trying to shake the memory.

I don't want to think of that, she whispered to herself. *I want something better to remember. Something finer.*

Her gaze slipped sideways.

William's hands gripped the reins loosely, his posture relaxed yet watchful. His jaw was set, the sun warming the clean line of his profile. He wasn't a poetic man. He wouldn't speak of light and shadow, of longing or color.

But he saw the land. He cared for it. For his cattle. For the men who worked under him.

Perhaps even for me. The idea was both terrifying and thrilling.

What would it be like to be kissed by such a man? To be held close, not with force or hunger, but with a steadiness that promised protection and care? His kiss would be different. She was sure of it. It would not take but would give. It would not bruise but would heal.

A warmth crept into her cheeks, and she twisted to look out over the fields, pretending interest in the sway of the prairie grass. The cool morning air couldn't seem to chase away the heat rising in her.

Ah, Keely Boyle. You'd best get your thoughts turned another way. Dreamin' of kisses from the likes of William Overstreet will only lead to heartache.

Even so, the dream lingered. Quiet and sweet. And she couldn't quite wish it away.

About an hour into the journey, William cast a glance over his shoulder and saw Victoria dozing, her head resting lightly on Roger's chest. No wonder his friend had fallen silent, the moment too sweet to disturb. Roger cradled his wife, one arm draped around her as though she were the most precious thing in the world.

William, on the other hand, needed a bit of conversation or he would be the next one falling asleep. If he couldn't talk to Roger, he would talk to Keely. He turned his gaze in her direction. "Did you rest well last night?" The question felt clumsy the moment it left his mouth, but he let it stand.

"Well enough."

He inhaled slowly, then tried again. "Tell me a bit more about yourself."

"Meself?" She looked at him in genuine surprise, the word lilting with that soft Irish melody he'd come to recognize and, if he was honest, appreciate more than he ought.

"Yes, I want to know more. I know you're an only child and that you lost both your parents and went to England after your mother passed. I know you worked at Hooke Manor for over a dozen years." He looked over at her. "But that's just a sketch."

"I wouldn't be thinking there's much worth telling."

He chuckled softly. "I suspect there's a great deal more to you, Miss Boyle, than a list of a few facts."

Her eyes widened. They were remarkable eyes. He'd always thought so. The same green found in deep forest shadows, both enchanting and unsettling in intensity. As for her heart-shaped mouth—

He turned back toward the road, his voice softer. "All right, then. Tell me something from your childhood."

There was a long pause. Was she afraid to share with him? But what had she to be afraid of? He only wanted to know her better. Maybe he should go first.

"When I was about nine," he said, "I decided I was old enough to prove I could handle real responsibility. I remember it was hot as all get out that day when I took it upon myself to 'help' with the horses. Of course, I didn't tell anyone what I planned to do."

He went on to explain how he'd tried to sneak one of the gentler mares out of the corral, only to spook her when he stumbled over uneven ground. "She bolted straight through the open gate, sending me scrambling after her, shouting and waving my hat as if that might help. By the time my father and two ranch hands caught up with us, the mare was happily rolling in the creek and I was soaked to the bone trying to coax her out of the water."

Keely laughed softly.

"I was sure I'd be in terrible trouble, but my father just laughed—after he made certain I was unhurt—and told me that growing up often looks like falling down first." William gave Keely a sideways glance. "I reckon we all carry a few such stories with us. Maybe you got into a bit of mischief yourself?"

She was quiet a short time longer before saying, "I don't know if you'd be calling it mischief, exactly, but there was the time I near drowned meself in the River Suir." Her voice carried a wistful note. "I was no more than eight. Da warned me more times than I could count to stay away from the river's edge. But it was a soft day, and I found a branch just right for pokin' about in the reeds. I leaned too far and slipped in. I can still feel the shock of the water closin' over me head. Cold as death."

He stiffened, imagining her slight frame swallowed by the current.

"Da heard me screams and came runnin'. Pulled me out by the scruff like a half-drowned pup." She gave a soft, breathy laugh. "I coughed and sputtered near to bursting. Mam wrapped me in every blanket we had. They scolded me fierce, but I saw the fright in their eyes. After that, I never went near the river alone again."

"Thank God for that," he said.

She glanced at him, half-smiling. "Now 'tis your turn to tell me another."

"You want another story from me?"

"Aye, that I do."

He grinned. "All right then. Let's see. I have plenty of them. Hmm." He rubbed his jaw, as if needing to give it a lot of thought. "When I was about eleven, Jocelyn and I got it into our heads we'd turn one of the ranch dogs into a circus pony."

Her brows lifted. "A dog?"

He chuckled. "Old Buster. Great shaggy brute, part wolfhound, we think. Big as a bear, loyal as the sun, and patient as any saint. Jocelyn decided he was just the right size to ride. So we borrowed one of Mother's kitchen towels for a saddle blanket, and I made a halter out of rope."

He could still picture Buster as plain as day.

"His legs were too long for his body, and he had a chest broad enough to knock a man off balance if he came barreling in too fast. His coat was a tangle of gray and black with streaks of rusty brown, rough as old rope no matter how often Jocelyn tried to brush him smooth. His ears never quite matched—one flopped, the other stood half-cocked—and his muzzle was grizzled even when he was young. For all that, he was as loyal as the sunrise and patient to a fault."

Keely smiled at William, waiting for him to continue.

"We got Jocelyn on his back for all of two seconds before he took off across the yard."

"The dog truly was big enough to ride?" she asked, incredulous.

"He was. But not agreeable. Jocelyn tumbled off into the hay, laughing so hard she couldn't breathe. Mother came out looking grim as thunder, arms crossed. However, when she saw Jocelyn was uninjured, she burst out laughing too. I think we had to do extra chores that week, but we didn't care. It was fun while it lasted."

Keely laughed outright, the sound bright and unguarded. It slipped past his defenses and caught him square in the chest.

He looked over at her again. The morning sun had brought out the copper tones in her hair curling upon her back. She had tied it at the nape with a yellow ribbon rather than attempting to tame it into a bun. He liked it that way.

She caught his eye and smiled, and something unstated passed between them.

He cleared his throat. "Speaking of animals with a mind of their own, Mrs. Adler mentioned Rowdy's kitchen escapade."

The smile dropped from her face. "Sure and he's not in any real trouble, is he?"

"No."

Her eyes narrowed just a little. "And me? Is she holdin' it against me?"

He grinned. "No. I promise. At least, I won't hold it against you . . . if you tell me another story from Ireland."

She lifted her chin, mock solemn. "I'm supposin' I could do that. Although I was such a dutiful child, I wasn't gettin' into much trouble."

For a heartbeat, he believed her. Then she laughed, a twinkle back in her eyes, and he suspected that, if he kept pressing her, she might have enough stories to entertain him all the way to Blackfoot and home again.

Chapter Eighteen

William left the hotel in Blackfoot on Friday morning, his boots striking a steady rhythm on the dusty boardwalk as he made his way toward the grange hall at the edge of town. For the past three days, he had thought little about the Teton Stock Growers' Association meeting, especially once he'd gotten Keely to tell him stories from her childhood. But now he was eager to talk with the other cattlemen about several pressing issues.

He rolled his shoulders back and lengthened his stride. Today, the purpose of the trip came front and center.

The grange hall stood plain and square against the morning light, built of sun-bleached timber with a front porch and a hitching rail already crowded with saddle horses. The air buzzed with flies, and the dust stirred beneath wagon wheels. Ranchers had come from miles around. He recognized a few of the wagons with the familiar brands scorched into the wooden panels.

Inside, the hall was dim, thick with the mingled scents of tobacco, sweat, and leather. Coats brushed shoulders as men moved to find space on the long benches, hats either pushed back or hung on rusted nails near the door.

He spotted Timothy Sanders near the front, the man's son Larry beside him, already deep in conversation with Major Hasting. The Overstreets and the Sanders family had been good neighbors for nearly twenty years. Most years, they drove cattle to the rail yards in Pocatello together. The hands shared campfires and watch shifts. Timothy Sanders, now in his late fifties, was a rough man but decent. His language unfit for Sunday company, perhaps, but his handshake was as strong as his word.

The Hasting Ranch was even farther to the south, but William knew the major well and respected him a great deal. In his late sixties, he had a full beard and bushy eyebrows, all of his hair thick and white as snow. He looked as wise as he actually was.

William gave a brief nod as he passed his neighbors, claiming a seat midway along one wall. The scrape of chairs and the low rumble of voices filled the room until a gavel cracked against the table.

"Order, gentlemen. Let's have order."

The president of the association, a gray-bearded man from the Henry's Fork country, stood at the head table. Beside him, a secretary with ink-stained fingers prepared to take down every word. The roll was called, names of ranches as much as men, and William answered when Eden's Gate was spoken. Then came the reading of the minutes from the last meeting, followed by reports—one man speaking of wolves troubling calves near St. Anthony, another complaining of sheep herds edging too close to cattle range along the Lost River. The usual tensions. The usual worry.

When the floor opened for new business, the tone shifted.

One man stood, hat in hand, demanding stricter regulations for recording brands, arguing that too many strays disappeared without explanation. Another raised the idea of hiring a new stock detective, stirring words of both agreement and resistance. The memory of rustlers —and the chaos they brought—hadn't faded.

William waited, listening. Measuring. Then, when the moment was right, he stood. A dozen heads turned his way.

"Gentlemen," he began, "I've no wish to raise alarm without cause. But I'd be wrong to keep quiet."

The silence told him he had their full attention.

"Last week, I found close to two dozen head at Eden's Gate sickened at a watering hole on my property. They've since recovered, thank the Lord, but I can't shake the thought that it wasn't natural. A witness saw a man, likely a stranger, at that same hole not long before the illness took hold. What he did there, I don't know. But the timing sits too close for comfort."

Murmurs broke the silence temporarily.

"I've checked everything else. The grass was healthy. No carcass upstream. No obvious signs of spoilage or contamination. But the water was the one common factor. And if this was intentional . . ." He paused, letting the weight of his words settle over the room. "Then it's not just my cattle at risk. Any of us could be next."

A man near the front let out a curse under his breath.

The president leaned forward, elbows braced on the table, gaze sharp. "You believe someone tampered with your water?"

William didn't flinch. "I believe it'd be foolish to dismiss the possibility. I've no hard proof, only suspicion. But in our line of work, suspicion's sometimes all you get before real trouble shows up."

From somewhere near the back, a voice asked, "Anyone else seen anything strange?"

Heads turned. No one spoke.

After a moment of silence, conversation swelled—overlapping voices, theories, and unease. The secretary struggled to keep pace, scribbling notes as fast as he could dip his pen.

The president rapped the gavel once more. "If no one else has a similar report, we'll treat this as a warning. Keep your eyes sharp. Especially for strangers nosing where they've no business."

William nodded and reclaimed his seat, jaw tight.

It wasn't a decisive action. He hadn't expected one. Not without actual evidence. But it was something. And now at least, the seed was planted. If anything else happened—at Eden's Gate or beyond—men would remember today.

After three days of riding in a wagon, jostled over rutted roads, Keely's muscles begged for motion. Her legs were stiff, her back ached from the unyielding bench, and her spirit was restless from so much idleness. She needed air and space.

So, after eating lunch with Victoria and Roger at the little restaurant across from the hotel, she declared her intention to take a walk. The day was fine. Warm without being stifling, a whisper of breeze stirring the leaves, and just a scattering of clouds across a sky so blue it made her throat ache to look at it.

"You shouldn't go alone," Victoria said firmly as they crossed back to the hotel. "You don't know this place. You could get turned around or worse. Roger, you ought to go with her."

"What about you?" he asked, already frowning.

"I'm going to lie down. I'm bone tired, and my back's been giving me twinges again."

"I'm not leaving you alone if you're not well."

Victoria gave a little shake of her head. "I'm perfectly well, darling. Truly. Simply tired."

At that moment, William appeared on the board-walk, his stride long and sure as he approached. At the sight of them, he raised a hand in greeting and quickened his pace.

As he drew closer, Roger asked, "How was the meeting?"

"Good. Nothing too unexpected."

"We just had lunch across the street. Are you needing something to eat?"

"No, they served lunch at the meeting." His gaze

flicked briefly to Keely, then returned to Roger. "Better than the boarding house in Rexburg. Not as good as anything Chuck prepares."

Roger nodded. "Keely wants to take a walk. But Victoria and I don't think she should go alone."

William didn't hesitate. His eyes came back to hers and stayed there this time. "Then I'll go with her. I could do with some fresh air myself. The fellow sitting next to me never let his cigar go out all morning. My lungs are in protest."

Keely's heart fluttered. Something had changed between her and William during the journey to Blackfoot. They had become . . . closer. Their manner had become . . . easier. Perhaps they had become friends. Although, in her heart, she knew she wanted William to be more than a friend.

"Shall we, Miss Boyle?" He extended his arm.

She hesitated a heartbeat before taking it. "Thank you." She nearly added his name, nearly said *William*, but the word caught in her throat.

They left the bustle of Main Street behind—the slap of horseshoes on hard-packed dirt, the creak and rattle of wagons, the coarse calls of men outside the livery. Out beyond the shops and the clapboard homes, the town gave way to open land. Grass swayed in the breeze. A meadowlark called somewhere off to the right, its song rising and falling.

"Blackfoot's smaller than I expected," Keely said at last.

"It's no grand city, that's true. But it's the county

seat, and that gives it importance. Most of the legal business in the county flows through here."

"Do you come to Blackfoot often?"

"At least once a year for the stock growers' meetings."

She nodded slowly. "I'm thinking I like Gibeon more."

Wordlessly, he pressed her hand against his side, as if to tell her he agreed.

Her gaze swept the land before them. Sagebrush dotted the dry earth, gray-green and tenacious, and farther off, dark rows of crops cut lines across the soil. A farmer had brought order here, coaxed life from hard ground. It was so different from the lush hills of Ireland or the soft manors of England. And yet her heart stirred.

Was this what belonging felt like?

She turned toward William, the question rising to her lips . . . then her toe caught on a half-buried stone, and the thought fled as she stumbled. She gave a small cry, her balance thrown.

Before she could fall to the ground, his arm wrapped firm around her waist and drew her upright. She landed against him, breath caught, heart hammering.

Time stilled.

His face was so close. She saw the flecks of gold in his eyes and felt the warmth of his breath upon her skin. His hands stayed at her waist. If he bent only an inch, his mouth would be on hers. Her lips parted in anticipation. She couldn't breathe, couldn't move, couldn't think.

But he didn't kiss her.

Slowly, gently, he helped her stand upright again,

letting his hands fall away. "You're all right," he said, voice thick.

"Yes, I'm fine, so I am."

Neither of them moved for a moment. Then they turned, step for step, and made their way back toward town. The silence between them was no longer companionable, but dense with unspoken things. Her pulse still raced, her lips tingled with what might have been.

She did not look up at him, but every part of her was aware of him. Of what he'd done. And what he hadn't.

Chapter Nineteen

Life quickly returned to normal after William and the others came back from Blackfoot. With no reports of cattle sickening elsewhere and the herd at Eden's Gate remaining healthy, he wondered if his instincts had been wrong. Perhaps he'd misjudged things. Maybe the cows falling ill soon after Keely had seen a man near the watering hole had been a mere coincidence. Nothing more. Or maybe she'd even been mistaken about what she thought she saw.

A week had passed since the stock growers' meeting, and though his hands held the reins and his eyes swept the hills for signs of strays, his thoughts were not on cattle. Not sick cattle. Not any cattle.

His thoughts were on Keely Boyle. Again. As they so often were.

So, no, life wasn't back to normal. Not entirely.

He leaned forward in the saddle, one forearm resting across the worn leather of the saddle horn. Then, with a shift in his seat, he sat up straighter and pressed his heels lightly to Skunk's sides. The stallion responded with a willing step, moving out at a steady walk along the creek that wound toward the foothills.

He'd nearly kissed her. There, on that quiet road outside Blackfoot, with her breath caught and her eyes lifted to his. He'd *wanted* to kiss her. *Still* wanted to.

She would've welcomed it. He'd been certain of that in the moment. And yet . . . Perhaps that was only what he wanted to believe. Perhaps what he'd seen in her eyes hadn't been an invitation at all, but confusion. Or longing for something she wasn't ready to trust.

Victoria had told him what had happened at Hooke Manor. How Keely had fled because of a man's unwanted attentions. A man of status. A man who believed himself untouchable. She'd feared no one would believe her if she spoke the truth. Hadn't he witnessed that very thing back in New York?

And what of himself? He was her employer. The man who'd given her shelter. Food. Respect. Wasn't it his duty to ensure she felt safe, not surprised by something she hadn't asked for? If he'd kissed her, would it have been with tenderness? Or would it have been taking advantage?

The questions scraped at him.

He wanted her to trust him. He wanted her to feel safe. And yet, the truth was he hadn't been thinking about trust or safety when he'd held her in his arms. He'd been thinking of her mouth. Of the warmth of her body. Of how perfectly she'd fit against him.

He'd wanted more than a kiss.

He grimaced and looked to the sky, as though the clarity of the open air might settle something inside him.

The old Scripture came back to him, half-remembered but sharp: *"But if they cannot contain, let them marry: for it is better to marry than to burn."*

He exhaled roughly. It had been a long time since he'd given any real thought to marriage. He'd celebrated other men's weddings, raised a toast or two, even danced when it was required. But after Violet, after her rejection, he'd decided solitude was easier. Safer.

Until Keely.

"Sweet sufferin' cats!" The familiar exclamation echoed in his mind.

He could see her clearly, as though she rode beside him, her eyes wide with amusement, her hands moving as she spoke, her hair escaping its ribbon no matter how carefully she tried to tie it back. That glorious hair, a riot of flame and copper, refused to be tamed. Just like her.

He nudged Skunk into a lope, needing to feel the rush of wind against his face, needing to think of something other than a woman who had taken up a place in his thoughts, in his life, with ease. But the faster he rode, the more she stayed with him.

Her laughter.

Her blush.

And he didn't know what to do about it.

Sweet sufferin' cats, indeed.

As Keely washed the last of the dishes, her gaze drifted to the few remaining slices of cooked meat on the work-table. Temptation stirred. She could wrap them in a napkin, slip them into her apron pocket, and carry them back to the cottage. Just in case.

It wasn't as though she went hungry at Eden's Gate. There was always more than enough food on the table. For that matter, she hadn't lacked for meals at Hooke Manor either. But that fear—the deep, gnawing fear of doing without—still lingered. A fear that hunger might find her again if she wasn't careful.

"Hey, Keely," Chuck called from across the kitchen, making her jump.

Guilt bloomed warm on her cheeks as she turned toward him.

"When you're finished there," he said, wiping his hands on a towel, "why don't you take some time for yourself? Mrs. Adler's gone for the afternoon, and I've got nothing for you to do. Go for a walk. Read a book. Do something that's just for you."

"Are you sure you won't be needing me?"

"I'm sure."

"Well then, I'll be going."

She dried the last pot and returned it to the shelf, then untied her apron and hung it on a hook near the door. A moment later, she slipped out the back, letting the screen door creak and clap behind her.

Rowdy was there almost instantly, his paws scrambling over the dirt path, tail wagging wildly.

"Hello, you." She leaned down to stroke his head.

"What shall we do with ourselves then, now that the afternoon's our own?"

She lifted a hand to shade her eyes from the sun, squinting toward the eastern pasture. No ranch hands were in sight, but it wasn't just any man she searched for.

It was William.

Always William.

Even when she told herself not to think of him—especially then—his face came to her mind. A smile. A glance. That steady voice that could rattle her and soothe her all at once. She didn't understand how it had happened, only knew that it had. He filled her thoughts, haunted her dreams, unsettled her heart.

Never in her life had she felt this way. She longed to be near him, and yet when she was, knots twisted her insides. Her emotions tossed her from joy to despair and back again like a paper boat caught in a storm. She wanted to speak the truth of her heart, but the fear of what he would say in return held her tongue. If he didn't feel the same . . .

Her chest tightened at the thought.

"I love him," she whispered, barely able to believe she'd said the words aloud.

Rowdy circled back to her, tongue hanging sideways from his mouth, ears perked as if he'd understood.

Louder this time, she said again, "I *love* him."

She dropped to her knees and took the dog's face between her hands, the truth in her voice now thick with aching. "But what can come of it, Rowdy? What could ever come of it?"

The dog whimpered, as if sharing the hopelessness

that rushed through her at the question. A question she'd refused to ask herself for the past week—ever since the moment William almost kissed her and the world had shifted beneath her feet.

With his thoughts still full of Keely, William at first assumed the woman and dog he saw in the distance were figments of a distracted mind. But no. It was Keely. Walking through the sagebrush, her hands moving in animated rhythm as she spoke to Rowdy trotting alongside her.

He grinned. Gestures almost always accompanied her words. Sometimes grand. Sometimes subtle. They were part of her language, as natural to her as the Irish lilt in her voice. And he wished he could know what she was saying.

He reined Skunk toward her and cantered down the slope. The moment she spotted him, she halted. Her hands stilled and pressed against her middle. Rowdy sat at her side.

William's pulse pounded in his ears, louder even than the drum of hooves beneath him. As he drew closer, he realized how much more beautiful Keely looked in the flesh than in any image his mind had conjured. And it felt like a lifetime since he'd been in her presence.

For it is better to marry than to burn.

He brought Skunk to a sudden stop, dirt spraying

beneath the stallion's hooves. In one swift movement, he swung down from the saddle.

Keely stood rooted in place, eyes wide with uncertainty, her left hand resting lightly on Rowdy's head. Whether to calm the dog or herself, he couldn't be sure.

"Keely Boyle," he said, voice rougher than intended.

"Aye," she whispered.

"There's something I want to say to you."

"Sir?"

He stepped closer. "I've given this a great deal of thought." The words caught in his throat. His mouth felt dry as a bone. He pressed his tongue to the roof of his mouth, searching for moisture, then forged ahead. "Keely . . . I believe we should get married."

She stared at him, clearly stunned. Her wide green eyes searched his face. "Sweet sufferin' cats," she breathed.

The first time he'd heard her whisper those words, he'd thought them odd. But they seemed to express this moment better than any other words he could think of.

He pulled off his Stetson with one hand, raking the other through his hair. "I know we don't know each other all that well. I know there's no love between us. But there's the start of a friendship. And people have built good marriages on less than that. Right?"

"I . . . I wouldn't be knowing, Mr. Overstreet."

Another step brought him closer. "I would be good to you, Keely."

"Sure and you've always treated me kindly. There's no denying that." Her voice was quiet, even, but her head shook slowly. "But that's still no reason for us to be wed."

The words struck deeper than he expected. Was she turning him down? Another rejection?

But this wasn't like before. This wasn't Violet Van Tress with her silks and fine breeding and a heart that never truly belonged to him. This was Keely, an orphan with barely more than the clothes on her back. A woman who cherished simple things. A woman who had, by all signs, grown to love Eden's Gate.

So why not him?

"Mr. Overstreet," she said softly, "why would you be wantin' to marry the likes o' me?"

It was a fair question.

And one he struggled to answer. At least, not with the honesty she deserved. Because though he'd claimed to have thought it through, he really hadn't. Not beyond the desire that burned within him. The need to hold her. Kiss her. Possess her.

She stepped back, her eyes darting over his face. Maybe she saw it there, the physical yearning he hadn't meant to reveal. "I could not, sir."

He took two steps forward, driven by instinct and the desperation to make her see that it could work, to convince her that marriage would suit them both.

"Please, Mr. Overstreet. No." Her words were faint, breathless, perhaps frightened.

Husbands, love your wives, even as Christ also loved the church, and gave himself for it.

The Scripture rolled through his mind. He wasn't her husband. But if he wanted to be, shouldn't he already be acting like one? Loving her in such a way that his first thought was to protect her, not claim her? Shouldn't cherishing her mean more than desire? It should mean sacrifice.

Slowly, he backed away, torn in two between wanting what he wanted and knowing what was right. "I'm sorry," he said quietly. "I didn't mean to frighten you."

"I am not frightened."

But she was. Her eyes told the truth.

He backed away another step. "I'll leave you to enjoy your walk in peace."

He inclined his head in respect, replaced his hat, turned, and mounted Skunk. Without another word, he rode away.

Chapter Twenty

Why did I do it?

As the first light of dawn crept into the cottage bedroom, Keely rolled onto her side, eyes fixed on the curtained window, uncertain whether she was thankful or sorry that the sleepless night had ended.

Why did I say no?

He had asked her to marry him. And she had refused.

"I know there's no love between us."

But he'd been wrong about that. She loved him. Well and truly. Even if he didn't love her in return.

"But there is the start of a friendship."

She was thinking he was right about that. Yes, he was her employer, but he'd never treated her like a servant. Bit by bit, they'd become something closer to friends.

"And people have built good marriages on less than that."

Sure and he was right about that, too. Would it really have been so terrible if she'd said yes?

"I didn't mean to frighten you."

He hadn't frightened her. Not in the way he meant. It was her own feelings that alarmed her. She longed for him with a fire that burned from the inside out.

Lord Jesus, help me.

Her mam had always said she could turn to the Blessed Savior in times of need. And if ever there was a time of need, surely this was one.

She slipped from beneath the covers and knelt beside the bed, the morning chill wrapping around her. With clasped hands on the mattress and her forehead bowed low, she whispered, "God Almighty, I'm a wretched sinner, that I am. I've done things I'm sore ashamed of. I've lied, and I've taken what isn't mine. But me mam said You'd forgive me if I turned to You and turned from me wrong-doing. So here I am, Lord. Turning. Forgive me. Help me know what I'm to do, for I surely don't know on me own. Jesus, I need You now. Amen."

She remained there, still and waiting. Waiting for clarity to fall like sunlight through glass. Waiting for wisdom to bloom inside her like a sudden spring. But no answer came. Not about William Overstreet. Not about what she ought to do next. And yet . . . something was different. Subtle, but sure. A quiet sense of being seen. Heard. Loved.

She lifted her head and opened her eyes. A strange peace had taken root inside her. It wasn't the certainty she'd hoped for, but it was enough. God cared. Just as her mam had always said. He cared about her troubles. He loved her, even after all she'd done wrong.

Maybe that was all she needed to know for now.

She rose, reaching for the robe Mrs. Adler had given her weeks ago. It hung too loose at the shoulders but held in warmth, and she pulled it close as she made her way into the parlor to stoke the fire.

Rowdy stirred from the rug near the door and padded over to her. He bumped his muzzle against her hand, tail swishing low.

"Hello, you rascal." She crouched to ruffle his ears. He wriggled in delight, front paws dancing, mouth parted in a toothy grin. Mrs. Adler insisted dogs couldn't smile, but Keely saw proof to the contrary every single day.

When the room was no longer cold, Keely washed up and dressed for the day. She wrestled the brush through her curls that refused obedience, then pinned what she could into place beneath her cap. Wisps sprang free the moment she turned from the mirror.

How she envied women with smooth, shining braids or golden waves that fell just so. But God had seen fit to give her Da's hair, just as ungovernable as the man had been. Only he had kept his hair cropped short. Lucky him.

With a sigh, she stepped into her boots and, after hooking the buttons, made her way outside.

Half an hour later, Keely carried a dented tin pail toward the chicken yard. Grain rattled with each step, and the hens, clever creatures that they were, came running the instant she lifted the latch. Wings flapped, feathers ruffled, and their eager clucking rose like a chorus.

"There's enough for all of you," she scolded with a

laugh, casting the feed in a broad arc. Golden kernels scattered over the packed earth, and the hens fell on them in a feathered frenzy.

One bold red hen darted between her boots. "Impudent thing. You'll be after tripping me yet," she warned, nudging it gently aside with her skirt.

She leaned against the fence for a moment, watching them scratch and bustle. Their feathered backs gleamed russet, white, and black in the morning light, and the steady rhythm of their contented clucks soothed something inside her.

A rooster crowed from the far corner. Keely shook her head. "You've missed your chance, sir. The dawn's long gone."

With the pail now empty and the hens scratching, she gathered eggs from the nest boxes, cradling the warm treasures in her apron. Mr. Kincaid would have them fried up within the hour.

She brushed a stray curl from her cheek with the back of her hand and glanced toward the big house, its windows catching the morning sun.

And for one sweet moment, the sense of belonging welled inside her again. The feeling she'd known only here, at Eden's Gate.

"This would be me home forever if I were to marry him."

True enough.

But she'd said no.

And now it was surely too late.

From the corner windows of his second-floor bedchamber, William watched Keely as she fed the chickens and gathered the morning's eggs. He saw the way she paused and looked up toward the house, lips moving with some quiet remark. Talking to herself? To the chickens? Or to Rowdy, who waited—tail thumping and ears alert—just outside the chicken yard fence?

Perhaps all three.

A soft chuckle escaped him despite the tired ache behind his eyes. That was Keely. She could make him laugh, even after a sleepless night spent wrestling with regret.

Or maybe it wasn't Keely who had kept him awake. Maybe it was the Lord Himself, stirring up his spirit and not letting him rest. Somewhere between midnight and dawn, a truth had broken through the fog of his uncertainty: love was not merely a feeling. It was an action. A decision. If he wanted to marry Keely—and he did, that hadn't changed—then shouldn't he begin by loving her now? Not waiting for emotion to dictate his steps, but choosing the path of care and devotion, whatever might come.

She had refused his proposal. That still smarted. But why had it surprised him? Despite a burgeoning friendship, there was much more he wanted to know about her and more that he wanted to share with her. As for the way he'd proposed, abrupt and graceless, with no tenderness and none of the words a woman might long to hear, no wonder she'd declined. He'd presented it more like a business transaction than a declaration of the heart.

That's what came of living as he had. Years spent in the saddle, surrounded by cattle and cowhands. He'd grown content in solitude, content in silence. Even as he'd watched friends like Sebastian and Jocelyn, Roger and Victoria, Amanda and Isaiah find love, he'd remained on the sidelines. Romance? It had seemed a chapter already closed. That door had slammed shut years ago, and he hadn't tried to open it again.

Had he let that mindset shape other parts of his life? Had he made it a habit—fail once, and never try again?

No, that wasn't the kind of man he was. He'd always been willing to try again, to reevaluate, to learn what needed changing. And if that was true for cattle and land and the men who worked for him, then it could be true for his own stubborn heart.

Outside, Keely stepped from the chicken yard, her apron full of eggs, Rowdy bouncing at her heels. He smiled again at the sight, then turned away from the window, resolve filling his chest. If giving up wasn't his way in the rest of his life, it wouldn't be his way with Keely Boyle either.

By the time his right boot hit the bottom step, he'd decided. He wouldn't be riding out to the range today. He'd be staying close to home.

And he would see what needed to be changed next.

Chapter Twenty-One

Later that afternoon, Keely carried a stack of freshly ironed shirts up to William's bedchamber. As always, she paused in the doorway to take in the room.

It was spacious, with tall windows facing east, north, and west. A massive four-poster bed stood against the lone interior wall, its carved posts rising like pillars. A bear rug sprawled near the fireplace—teeth bared, mouth forever open in a snarl that made her shiver every time she looked at it.

This would be me bedroom if I were to marry him.

Och, she was daft for certain. Soft in the head. To keep having thoughts like that, about this house, about this room. She'd refused William's offer. That should've been the end of it. No going back now.

Drawing a breath to steady herself, she crossed to the chiffonier, opened one of the middle drawers, and laid the shirts inside with careful hands. These were his fine shirts, the ones he wore with a suit to church or to meetings like the one in Blackfoot. He always looked handsome in them, of course. But in her heart, she loved the sight of him in his work clothes more.

She could see him clearly in her mind—broad shoulders filling out a worn chambray shirt, the sleeves rolled high to reveal strong, sun-browned forearms. His trousers were sturdy, dusted with the land he worked. His boots, well-worn and scuffed, told their own story of miles traveled and work well done. A vest sometimes adorned his frame, sometimes not. And always, his dark Stetson cast shadows across his brow, lending a quiet mystery to the eyes beneath.

It wasn't the cut of his clothes that stirred her. It was in how he wore them. The calm confidence, the strength in every motion, the way he seemed utterly himself in the wide, wild world.

"Keely."

She whirled at the sound of his voice. Had she conjured him from thought alone?

"I didn't expect you to be in here," he said.

Heat flushed her cheeks. "I was just putting away the ironing."

"I'm sorry if I disturbed you."

"You didn't, sir."

A lie, of course. His presence always disturbed her. Disturbed her in a way that made her feel breathless, disoriented, undone. And yet she longed to be near him always.

"There's something I need to say," he continued, his tone quiet, measured. "I'm glad I found you alone."

Her gaze dropped to a knot in the floorboards.

"I want to speak about yesterday."

She held her breath.

"I won't pester you, Keely. I give you my word on that. But I'm not content to leave things as they are."

"Mr. Overstreet—"

"William," he said gently.

"I don't—"

"Friends use given names. We are friends. You agreed."

She looked up at last, hesitant. "Sir, I—"

"William," he said again. Gentle. Firm.

"William." Her voice was barely a whisper. "But Mrs. Adler won't be liking it."

That drew a genuine smile from him. "Let me worry about Mrs. Adler."

Sure and that was easy for him to say.

"There's a potluck tomorrow after church," he said. "Will you sit with me? I'll ask Roger and Victoria to join us."

Mrs. Adler would like that even less. What should she say? She had walked with him before, yes. Dined at Miss Irene's with him and others. Traveled beside him to and from Blackfoot. But this felt different. He had asked her to marry him. Perhaps not out of love, but he had asked. And she did love him, more with each passing day. What if someone guessed it? What if they saw what was in her heart?

A door slammed somewhere below, the sound sharp and sudden.

"Boss!" Tom's voice. Urgent.

William turned and went out to the top of the stairs. "What is it?" he called back.

"More sick cattle. And they're dyin' this time."

Without hesitation or a backward glance, William descended the stairs.

Keely moved to the doorway. *Wait*, her heart cried. But he was already gone. She followed as quickly as she could, but by the time she reached the landing and peered down into the parlor, both men had vanished.

The sharp scent of trampled grass and fear reached William's nose before he and Tom even reined in. Sage tossed her head, uneasy, her ears flicking at invisible flies. It didn't take long to see why.

Several steers lay sprawled on their sides, bellies bloated, legs thrashing weakly against the earth. One let out a ragged, broken bawl before its head jerked back, spine arching unnaturally. Foam streaked its muzzle, spattering the dirt.

"God in heaven," William muttered under his breath.

Jake Foster was already off his horse, hat in hand, his face pale. Mick Chandler stood near the edge of the pond, arms crossed, shoulders hunched, staring down at the water that lapped innocently against the bank, despite the havoc it had wrought.

"Boss," Jake said as William dismounted, "they began droppin' a little over an hour ago. First one started shiverin', then another. Now—" He swept his hand at the scene before them, helpless.

William strode forward, boots sinking into the soft ground. His stomach turned as he counted. Seven dead already. Five more in their last spasms. Two staggered in dazed circles, muscles twitching uncontrollably.

"This isn't the same as before," he said grimly.

Tom spat into the dirt. "No, sir. Last time they were sick, but they had a chance. These—" He shook his head. "These ain't comin' back."

William crouched beside a young steer, only two winters old. Its legs paddled uselessly. Its eyes were wide, white-rimmed, panicked. Chest heaving. He reached out, rested a hand on its neck, but could do nothing more. Moments later, the animal gave one last violent jerk and went still.

Rage coiled hot and tight in his chest. Illness didn't strike like this. Not so fast. Not so sudden. This wasn't natural.

Mick came up beside him, voice low. "You reckon it's the pond?"

William stood slowly, eyes sweeping the water's surface. It looked harmless. Only a few wisps of grass floating on the surface. But he didn't trust the look of it. Not anymore.

"Keep the rest of the herd well back," he said. "And don't let anyone touch that water. I don't know what's in it, but I'm not losing any of you to poison."

The crew was already moving, wrangling the herd northward, away from danger. William returned to Sage and mounted, casting a long look across the pasture. In the distance, beyond the fence line, lay the Sanders property. He needed to warn Timothy Sanders, and he would do it himself this time.

His gaze dropped again to the fallen steers. These cattle should've fattened over the summer and been shipped to market come fall. They represented years of investment and labor. Their deaths would echo in the ledgers long after this summer.

He reined Sage around. "Jake, I'm headed down to speak with Sanders. Move the herd to the upper range. Get them far away from South Creek."

Jake nodded. "I'll take care of it."

William tugged his hat lower and nudged Sage into a lope. About twenty minutes after passing through the gate onto Sanders's land, he came upon Timothy and two of his men. They sat astride their horses, all of them staring down into a gully. William reined in beside them and looked.

A steer lay below. Dead. No doubt about it. But it was alone. He scanned the pasture beyond. Healthy cattle grazed undisturbed.

"Overstreet," Timothy greeted, turning slightly in his saddle.

"Sanders." William tugged his hat. "Trouble?"

"A wolf, looks like. Judging by the tracks." Timothy gestured to the soft earth below. "Lucky they only got one."

William exhaled. Relief mixed with dread. "I was worried it might be worse."

"What brings you down this way?"

"I've got trouble too. Bad trouble. My cattle were poisoned again—different water source this time."

Timothy's expression darkened. "Same as before?"

"No. This is worse. They're not just sick. They're dying. Fast. About a dozen head dead already. It's the pond by the east pasture, the one fed by South Creek. Someone added something to it. I'm sure of it now. A different kind of poison this time is my guess."

Timothy cursed, his gaze scanning the horizon. "There ain't no way to keep eyes on every corner of a place the size of your ranch. Mine either. We all know it."

"We do." His tone was grim.

"Any idea who'd do such a thing?"

William shook his head slowly. He'd been asking himself the same question for days now. What would someone gain by it? Who stood to benefit from this kind of loss?

Killing a dozen cattle wouldn't break Eden's Gate. It would hurt his profit margin, yes. Might cause stress and suspicion. But not ruin. Not on its own.

Then what was the purpose?

His jaw clenched. He had a feeling he wouldn't sleep soundly again until he had an answer.

And even then, only if justice followed.

Chapter Twenty-Two

The next morning, Keely drove the buggy to church, feeling a measure of confidence holding the reins that she hadn't possessed weeks earlier. She was alone, save for a silent Mrs. Adler seated beside her. William and the ranch hands had remained behind, continuing to move the Overstreet cattle closer to the ranch complex where they could monitor the herd vigilantly in the coming days.

News of the poisoned cattle had already reached town, and it was the major topic of conversation at the potluck that followed the morning service. Ranchers were not the only ones concerned. It touched everyone. William Overstreet was well regarded, a friend and a good man, and Eden's Gate greatly contributed to the prosperity of the entire region.

"What are you gonna do about it, Sheriff?" a man Keely didn't know asked Frank Lewis.

"We'll do our best to find the man or men responsible," the sheriff replied. "You can be assured of that."

"They could be long gone by now," another said.

Reverend Blankenship, seated across from Keely at the far end of a long table, raised his voice above the quiet murmurs of those gathered. "Behold, your sins will find you out. Thus saith the Lord."

Her own sins—confessed just the morning before in whispered prayer—rose unbidden to Keely's mind. After a long silence, she leaned forward, her voice hushed. "Are you thinkin' that is always true, Reverend?"

"That our sins find us out?" His dark eyes held steady as they met hers. "Yes, Miss Boyle. I believe it is."

Although she judged the reverend's age to be not much more than her own, there was wisdom in his eyes and authority in his voice that made her trust him. Or at least want to trust him. "So whoever did this to Will—" She caught herself. "To Mr. Overstreet . . . will be caught. God promises that?"

He inclined his head slightly. "The Lord doesn't promise that evildoers will be discovered by our good sheriff or by any other man. That depends on God's will and His perfect plan. But unless our sins are covered by the blood of Christ, they will not go unseen by our Maker. Nor will they go unpunished."

Keely hesitated. "But if they *are* confessed . . . others won't find them out?"

He gave her a long look before leaning toward her. "That I cannot promise either. While confession and repentance bring us God's grace, that doesn't always mean we escape the earthly consequences of what we've done."

"Oh." She dropped her gaze to the nearly empty plate in front of her.

"Miss Boyle?"

She looked up again.

His voice was lower now, more personal. "I may be mistaken, but it seems to me you have some questions that would be better discussed in a quieter place than this."

Heat flared in her cheeks. Could she hide nothing from anyone?

"Would you mind if I called on you at the ranch one day this week?"

She wanted to say she'd be too busy, that her duties at Eden's Gate wouldn't allow time for such a visit. But that would be untrue, and she didn't want to lie again. Especially not to a man of God. "Of course, Reverend. If you'd like."

"I would like." He smiled warmly. "And I look forward to it." Then, perhaps taking pity on her, he turned to the man seated beside him and started a new conversation.

Keely glanced at Mrs. Adler, who was deep in discussion with another woman. Alone with her thoughts once more, she picked up her fork and speared the last bite of pie. As she chewed and swallowed, Victoria approached, stopping at the end of the table.

"Mrs. Adler? Excuse me for interrupting."

"That's perfectly all right, dear."

"Roger wonders if we might come to stay at Eden's Gate for a time. Since William isn't here today, I thought to ask you."

"Is something wrong at your home?" the house-keeper asked.

"Not at all. Roger just wants to lend a hand to William for as long as he's needed. But he doesn't want me staying in town alone."

"Heavens! Of course he doesn't." Mrs. Adler gave an approving huff. "You know we have more than enough room for you. Of course, you may come. Come today if you wish. We'll be ready for you."

Victoria turned her smile upon Keely. "I have so many fond memories of my time on Eden's Gate before Roger and I married."

A twinge of jealousy stirred inside Keely. William and others had welcomed Victoria as a guest, while they'd brought Keely on as a housemaid. But she dismissed the thought almost at once. Their circumstances—hers and Victoria's—had been undeniably different.

"'Twill be good to have you there," she said—and meant it.

"Wonderful. Then we'll come later this afternoon." With a graceful turn, Victoria moved away.

Mrs. Adler chuckled softly. "This will be interesting."

Keely glanced at her, brow raised. "What do you mean?"

"Mr. Bernhardt is no cowboy, that's all. He's got a good heart, and Mr. William will appreciate whatever help he can give. But keeping watch over a place as big as Eden's Gate isn't easy work. Still . . ." She let the rest of her thought trail off.

"Sure and I would help too, if I could."

Mrs. Adler reached over and patted her hand. "Of course you would, girl. I've no doubt of it."

From a ridge in the foothills, William watched as the Eden's Gate cattle streamed toward the northeastern section. The cow-and-calf herd moved in a slow, undulating line, hides glinting red-brown and white under the sun. Dust rose beneath thousands of hooves, drifting like smoke over the sagebrush. Now and again, a cow lifted her head and bawled for her calf, and the reply came, higher-pitched and urgent, half lost in the thunder of movement and the jangle of iron from the cowboys' tack.

Skunk tossed his head, ears flicking back and forth, and let out a sharp snort. He pawed the earth, restless from the motion and noise below. William steadied the horse with a hand on the reins, his eyes fixed on the herd as they pressed through the wide opening in the fence. Below him moved the living wealth of Eden's Gate, shifting from one range to another.

God, You alone know what the loss of those steers will do to the ranch. It hurts. It will cost us come fall. You alone know how I can keep it from happening again. How do I protect the rest of the cattle?

Anger churned in his chest. The financial loss mattered, but it wasn't the numbers that had kept him awake at night. It was the memory of those animals suffering—strong, healthy steers collapsing to the dirt, their limbs jerking, eyes rolling white, foam streaking their muzzles.

He was a practical man, but he wasn't without a heart. His cattle weren't just inventory. They were part of the responsibility—no, the trust—God had placed in his care. He had been called to steward this land and everything on it. Grass, water, horses, men, and cattle.

He tightened his grip on the reins, jaw locked. Whoever had done this hadn't just stolen from him. They had struck at his calling. Stewardship was more than a verse in the Good Book. It was written into his sweat, into every hour of labor, every decision made in the saddle or at the desk.

Did he know that, the one who did this? Was he a stranger? Or worse, a man William might have called a friend? Was it his aim to leave him sleepless, to fill his nights with the sound of dying cattle?

The thought turned his stomach. No. No, he hoped the man or men were strangers. It would be easier to bear.

Below, Jake broke from the herd and urged his mount up the slope toward him.

"Any problems?" William asked, though he could already tell there hadn't been.

Jake shook his head. "Nope. Cows and calves are through. We'll move the steers first thing in the morning."

"Who's watching them?"

"Logan's down there now. I'll send a couple more boys to join him once this bunch settles."

"Keep a close eye on the water."

"We will, boss."

William looked northeast, toward the trees. One of the creeks on the property flowed down from the forested hills beyond. He followed its curve with his eyes, tracing the unseen paths it cut through Eden's Gate. So much depended on those waters. Life, growth, survival. But water could carry death as easily as it carried life.

"We could use more men," Jake said.

"I know." William let out a breath. "I'll see to it tomorrow."

His foreman nodded once, then turned his horse and headed back down toward the herd.

William stayed where he was a moment longer, watching the last of the cows and calves pass through the fence opening, their shapes slowly swallowed by the dust. Then he turned Skunk and rode toward the ranch house —and the ledger books waiting on his desk. Numbers that didn't lie. Numbers that would tell him in plain terms the cost of this sabotage. More men, more mouths to feed, more wages to pay.

And summer had only just begun.

Chapter Twenty-Three

Standing in the shade of the trees between the barn and the house, Keely ran a brush along Duke's flank. A sense of satisfaction filled her. Upon returning from church with Mrs. Adler, she'd managed to unhitch the buggy and remove all the tack herself. A minor victory, but one she cherished. No men had been in sight. Even Chuck had disappeared for the afternoon.

"I'm hoping there's not been more trouble," she said aloud, glancing at Rowdy where he lay in the dirt near the hitching post.

The dog whimpered in response, then resumed licking his front paw. Keely bent to rub his ears, seeking comfort as much as offering it. Her eyes drifted toward the far range stretching to the mountains. Were the cattle safe? More importantly, was William safe?

She pressed the brush harder against Duke's side, trying to steady the tremble in her hand. William was strong and capable, well-accustomed to the burdens of the ranch. But he wasn't invincible. If she hadn't refused his offer of marriage, she might be beside him now, lending him her strength. He needed help. He needed comfort.

The rhythmic thud of hooves broke through her thoughts. She straightened, shading her eyes. Out of the drifting dust, a rider emerged—tall in the saddle, shoulders square. Relief flooded her so fast her knees went weak.

William.

He rode at a steady lope, slowing as he neared the barnyard. Sweat darkened Skunk's chest, and dust clung to William's shirt. Fatigue lined his face, but he sat straight, every inch the master of Eden's Gate.

Rowdy leapt to his feet and barked.

"Hush, boy," Keely commanded. "Sit."

The dog sidled closer before obeying.

"You got back from church all right, I see," William said as he dismounted.

"We did."

A weary smile tugged at the corners of his mouth. "And you've taken care of Duke all by yourself."

"I have." She smiled back, pleased he'd noticed.

"How was the potluck?"

"There was little talk besides what happened here."

"That doesn't surprise me." He walked closer.

"Mr. and Mrs. Bernhardt are coming to stay," she added.

He raised an eyebrow.

"Roger is wanting to be of help. They'll be here soon, I'm thinkin'."

His puzzled look shifted into a frown. "I won't turn down his help. I'm going to have to hire more men."

Studying his face, it seemed to her that he'd aged several years in the twenty-four hours since he'd stood in his bedchamber, asking if she would sit with him at the church potluck. She wanted to reach out and smooth the crease of worry from his brow. She wanted to tell him that all would be well, although she didn't know if that was true.

He stepped closer, almost within reach.

Without thinking, she dropped the brush and lifted her arms, wrapping them around his neck, drawing him close. Offering what little comfort she could with her embrace.

He didn't resist.

For a long moment, they simply stood there. Then a groan rumbled from his chest, and he whispered, "Keely."

Her name, wrapped in longing and weariness, pierced her heart.

She drew back just enough to look into his eyes. She didn't know how long she searched his face. Moments. Hours. And then, at last, he lowered his head. His lips brushed hers. Softly at first. Then deeper. Longer.

Her breath caught. Emotion surged within her, sharp and overwhelming. His hand cradled the back of her head, fingers tangling in her hair. The kiss stole her breath, stole her sense, stole everything as the world fell away.

There was only William.

Only this.

She barely registered the faint sound of an approaching buggy until William pulled away, his hands resting on her shoulders, holding her back.

"We've got company," he said quietly.

She drew in a steadying breath, feeling windblown and disheveled. Whoever was coming, they would surely know with one look at her what had happened. She grabbed the brush from the ground and stepped to Duke's side, hoping against hope that the gelding would hide her from everyone until her composure returned.

If it ever returned.

Amazing, wasn't it, how something as simple as a kiss could make William forget everything else in his world? Even the worst of it—poisoned cattle, financial loss, the shadowy unknown behind it all—had vanished from his mind the instant his lips met Keely's. As though none of it existed. As though only she did.

But now . . . now he remembered.

Clearing his throat, he took another step back as a horse and buggy rounded the corner of the barn. Just as Keely had said, Roger and Victoria had come. He forced a smile and raised a hand in welcome.

"I wasn't certain we would find you here," Roger called out, reining in the horse. "I imagined you would be far afield."

"I was. Only just rode in." He reached out to help

Victoria down. "Keely mentioned you plan to become one of my cowboys."

Roger chuckled as his boots hit the ground. "I daresay that would be an impossibility. You would have more success turning a sow's ear into a silk purse. However, I can sit a horse and follow instructions, and if you can use me, I am at your bidding."

William didn't laugh. "To be honest, my friend, I'm more than grateful. But what about your gallery? Your own work?"

"I am between commissions. And my gallery will keep. For all that I love about my new home, Gibeon does not boast the most enthusiastic patrons of the arts."

Victoria, glancing toward the trees, must have spotted Keely still brushing Duke. She murmured something to Roger and then walked that way, leaving the two men alone.

Roger's expression turned serious. "Be honest. How concerned are you?"

By quiet agreement, the two men walked toward the corral, out of earshot.

"Very concerned." William rested his forearms against the fence rail. "I keep going over everything in my mind, trying to figure out who would want to do this. To me. To Eden's Gate. Have I harmed someone without knowing? Have I insulted someone? Enough that they would want to do this?"

"You mustn't blame yourself. Someone else did this evil. That's on them, not you."

"But people don't act without a reason. Rustlers steal for money. That makes a kind of sense, even if it's wrong.

But this?" He shook his head. "What do they hope to gain from poisoning cattle?"

Roger laid a hand on William's shoulder. "I don't know. I wish I did."

They stood in silence, the warm hush of the afternoon pressing in around them.

Finally, Roger dropped his hand and straightened. "All right, then. Put me to work."

William turned from the corral and scanned the yard. Someone had led Duke away. Keely and Victoria, he supposed, had gone into the house.

The memory of Keely's arms around his neck, the feel of her kiss—her warmth, her willingness—flooded him anew. He longed to go to her. To talk. To kiss her again.

But now was not the time for pursuing romance. There were more important matters that demanded his attention. He'd returned to the ranch house to attend to his ledgers. After that would come a trip to the bank in the morning, followed by putting out the word that he was hiring and placing an order at the general store for more food and supplies.

"How's your arithmetic?" he asked Roger.

His friend gave him a sideways look. "Passable. Why?"

William tilted his head toward the house. "You'll see. Tomorrow, I'll put you in a saddle. But today . . ." He gave a wry smile. "Today, we do sums."

Keely sat on the edge of the mattress in her cottage bedroom, staring down at the brooch cradled in her hand.

So delicate. So lovely.

Jocelyn Whitcombe had worn it often, always pinned neatly at her collar. Each petal, fashioned from pale blue enamel, formed a perfect forget-me-not. A single seed pearl gleamed from its center, catching the light with a soft luster. Though small, the piece possessed a simple elegance. Time had softened its edges, dulled its shine, but it remained beautiful nonetheless.

Perhaps that was why Keely had kept it. Why she'd never been able to let it go. Even though it held no real value.

"Hardly worth a tuppence," she'd been told by the buyer when she'd surrendered the other pieces—the fine earrings, the diamond necklace, the delicate bracelet. Treasures she'd stolen. Not out of greed, but desperation.

She'd tucked the brooch away afterward. Hidden it. Brought it with her to America, across an ocean and into a life she never could have imagined.

Now, with the memory of William's kiss still warm in her heart, she wept. Wept over what she had done. What she could never undo. The tears slipped soundlessly down her cheeks as she closed her fingers around the brooch.

Please, God. Her thoughts choked on the words. *May William never know the truth.*

Chapter Twenty-Four

Feather duster in hand, Keely stepped into the parlor late Tuesday morning and came to an abrupt halt. Victoria sat on the settee near the window, reading glasses perched on her nose and a small book resting atop the swell of her belly.

"Oh. I beg pardon, Mrs. Bernhardt. I was meaning to dust but don't want to disturb you."

"You're not disturbing me, Keely." Victoria removed her spectacles and set them aside. "And I thought we'd agreed on first names. You must call me Victoria."

Keely offered a hesitant smile but said nothing.

"Why don't you come sit with me?" Victoria patted the settee. "Let's have a visit."

Keely glanced over her shoulder toward the kitchen. "I'm meant to be working."

"Mrs. Adler won't mind. She understands more than you might think."

"I don't know what you're meaning."

Victoria smiled gently. "My friend, you've become far

more than a maid in this house. Surely you understand that."

Keely shook her head, uncertainty tightening her lips.

"You really believe none of us have noticed the way you and William behave around each other?"

Heat rose in her cheeks. "I . . . you . . . we . . ."

Victoria laughed as she set the book next to her glasses. "Please, Keely. I'm dreadfully in need of company. I'm no longer used to spending so much time alone. The dusting can wait."

With a soft sigh, Keely gave in. She crossed the room and perched on the edge of the nearest chair, the duster still in her lap.

"Do you like to read?" Victoria asked, her fingers tapping the closed book beside her.

"I've never had much time for it."

"It's always been one of my favorite things to do. Though my eyes no longer appreciate the small print most books seem to favor." She rubbed the bridge of her nose. "And I've always hated having to wear spectacles. It's such a nuisance when I misplace them. And of course, vanity plays a part. I fear they make me look old." Her features softened into a smile. "Roger says he likes the look of them on me. He even wants to paint a picture of me wearing them, but I told him no."

"But if he insists, you will," Keely said with certainty.

"You're absolutely right. If he insists, I will. I am like putty in his hands." Smiling, Victoria laid a hand over her rounded belly. "But there will be no portrait painting until after this baby is born."

"How much longer must you wait?"

"Dr. Grant says about three months. Perhaps a little more."

Keely leaned forward slightly, curiosity pulling her in. "Were you always like putty in Mr. Bernhardt's hands?"

Victoria's eyes widened. "Oh, heavens, no. I resisted the idea of loving him, even when I knew I'd already lost that battle. Neither of us thought we could have a life together. He was determined to go wherever the wind blew him, painting whatever he pleased. And I planned to have a predictable and secure life, with both feet firmly planted. We thought we were all wrong for each other, our wants too different." She chuckled softly. "But God thought otherwise."

"Are you believing it was God who brought the two of you together?"

Victoria's expression sobered. "Yes, I believe it. It could have only been the Lord who orchestrated our meeting and our eventual union."

"Me mam believed like you. She used to say God cares about everything to do with us, big and small."

"And what do you believe, Keely?"

Lowering her gaze to the duster, she ran her fingers over the wooden handle, twirling it until the feathers fluttered softly across her skirt. "I maybe could believe it," she said at last, voice low.

"William likes you a great deal, you know."

Keely looked up, meeting Victoria's steady, knowing gaze. *He's never said as much*, she wanted to argue.

But the memory of his kiss silenced the words. Two days had passed, and still it lingered in her thoughts like an ember that refused to die. She could recall the feel of his arms around her, the strength of them, the warmth. She wanted to feel it all again. Only she was afraid. Afraid because William had kissed her without knowing everything about her, including her secret shame.

Victoria seemed to sense her inner struggle. "Whatever haunts you, Keely, I pray you'll find the strength to let it go."

She gave a faint nod, her throat tight.

After a moment, Victoria rose and crossed the room with care. She placed a hand on Keely's shoulder and gave it a gentle squeeze. "If ever you need to talk—to me or to the Lord—you don't need to wait." Then she turned and left the room, her soft footsteps fading into the quiet.

Keely remained where she sat, the duster resting still in her lap, and the ache of unexpressed truths swelling once again in her throat.

If William were honest with himself, he'd have to admit that Roger was proving more useful than expected. He couldn't rope at all, but he sat a saddle well and kept a sharp eye. Twice that morning, Roger had followed the creek from its origin in the foothills and back again, scanning for signs of trouble—tracks, tampered fences, anything to suggest someone had been near the water source with mischief in mind. So far, he'd reported nothing unusual and had just set out again for a third circuit.

William's gaze shifted to the herd of steers grazing in

the northernmost section of the ranch. They couldn't remain here forever. The forage was too thin. Eden's Gate might stretch for miles in all directions, but its pastures required constant rotation to keep the cattle fed, the land healthy, and the herd fattening toward market weight.

In the distance, he spotted Logan Coe riding along the fence line, his silhouette crisp against the horizon. Farther west, two more hands had paused to exchange a few words before moving on. At a glance, it might've passed for any ordinary day at the end of May, sun high, cattle calm, riders scattered across the land. But William knew better. This wasn't an ordinary day, and he couldn't pretend otherwise.

A flicker of movement at the edge of his vision drew his attention. Three riders were cantering in from the west, closing the distance fast. Not his own men, from what he could tell. He reined Sage around and waited, posture straight, hand resting lightly on the horn. As the riders neared, he recognized the one in the lead.

Brian Townsend. Victoria's brother, riding tall and confident, with two Hasting Ranch hands flanking him. William raised a hand in greeting.

"Brian," he called. "Good to see you."

Brian brought his horse to a halt, and the other men followed suit. "It's been a while."

"Too long. How's Kit? And the baby?"

"Both are doing well. Grayson's about to walk."

"No," he said, eyebrows rising. "Already?"

"About another month, so Kit tells me."

William shook his head. It seemed like only yesterday

Kit delivered Grayson in an upstairs room at Eden's Gate. But it wasn't yesterday. More like ten months ago.

"The major heard about the recent poisoning," Brian said. "Sent us to lend a hand. Said we're to stay as long as you need us."

A lump rose in William's throat, sudden and unexpected. There were good people in these parts. Neighbors who didn't wait to be asked before offering help. Major Hasting might be blunt and rough-edged, but his loyalty ran deep, and his word meant something.

He cleared his throat and nodded. "I appreciate it."

"We dropped off our gear at the bunkhouse before riding out." Brian gave a nod. "Just point us where you want us."

William looked around, scanning the land, the cattle, the open sky that stretched forever above them. He spotted Jake and gave a quick whistle. The foreman turned his horse and trotted over.

Within minutes, Jake had issued instructions, and the three Hasting cowboys headed south to check the other watering holes. William watched them go, grateful but still unsettled. He knew he needed more hands. And even with more hands, it might not be enough.

It was nearing the dinner hour when William loped Sage toward the ranch house. Several of the men had remained out on the range to keep watch over the herd for the night, a routine that would likely continue for the foreseeable future. Others would return to the bunkhouse to eat and catch a few hours of shuteye before heading out again at dawn. No one knew how long this arrangement would last. Even with the addition of the three cowboys sent by Major Hasting, Eden's Gate was still running shorthanded.

William could only hope the help-wanted notices he'd placed in both the Gibeon Weekly Times and a newspaper out of Pocatello would bring in enough responses. He needed at least five more men. Preferably ten. The trouble, of course, was that he couldn't offer long-term work, just temporary employment until he believed the danger was over. And for most cowboys, that made the job less than desirable.

As he approached the barnyard, he spotted Roger and Victoria seated together on the porch, deep in conversation. Then his gaze shifted—and there she was. Keely. She stood outside the guest cottage, bent at the waist in a tug-of-war with Rowdy, who pulled against an old scrap of cloth as if it were the greatest prize in the world and he meant to keep it.

A slow smile tugged at William's mouth. That dog would never be worth a lick on the range. In a matter of weeks, Keely had transformed the pup from a would-be working dog into a spoiled pet. Not that William could bring himself to care. There were bigger worries occupying his mind.

Keely straightened then, lifting her gaze in his direction. He felt it like an arrow to the heart.

Two days had passed since he'd kissed her. Thoroughly kissed her. She'd kept her distance ever since. He'd hardly seen her, and when he had, she'd managed to vanish before any actual conversation could happen. Even so, those brief encounters had been charged with something unsaid, something just beneath the surface. Out on the range, he could push her from his mind. But seeing her now, in the soft light of late afternoon, made everything else seem small by comparison. He knew that shouldn't be the case. But it was.

He dropped down from the saddle and tied Sage to the hitching post. But when he turned again, he didn't see Keely. A quick search discovered Rowdy lying by the back door, head on paws, and William knew she'd slipped away once again.

Did she regret the kiss that much?

He scrubbed a hand across his forehead. What a mess. He wanted to court her, to win her, to make her his wife. But he kept bungling it. At every turn, it seemed. Perhaps it was for the best. Heaven knew he had enough trouble on his hands without adding matters of the heart to the mix.

But then a thought struck him. Did he truly think loving Keely was a problem?

He frowned and laid a hand on Sage's shoulder, flipping the stirrup aside and reaching for the cinch. He was so caught up in thought, he didn't notice he was no longer alone until a quiet throat-clearing sounded from the opposite side of the horse.

Roger said, "Mrs. Adler will be glad you came in for supper after all."

William grunted in response and yanked the cinch free before lifting the saddle and blanket from Sage's back. He carried them to the rack, returned with a brush, and began to work the dust from the mare's flanks.

"Mind if I offer a bit of advice?" Roger asked.

"Depends on what it is. If it's about catching the man who poisoned my cattle, I'm all ears."

"It's not. It's actually something you once said to me."

That got William's attention. He paused mid-stroke and glanced over the horse's back.

"Last summer," Roger said, "when I was all tangled up in my feelings for Victoria, you told me, 'Don't you suppose you should talk to her about it?'" He smiled faintly. "I daresay you were right. And I think the advice still holds. It's time you spoke to Miss Boyle. Be honest with her about your feelings."

William turned back to brushing. "You don't know—"

"I know enough. I've got eyes." He flicked a glance toward the porch. "We've all got eyes."

"It's not as simple as just talking."

"Isn't it? I think it might be. And if it's not, then talking is at least a start."

"I'm her employer. That complicates matters."

"That's an excuse." Roger pinned him with a firm gaze. "And there's an answer to it. Make her a guest instead of an employee. She's living in your guest cottage already. You've got chaperones aplenty. Victoria, Mrs. Adler, half the ranch. You and I both know Mrs. Adler doesn't need Keely's help. She gives her tasks to keep her busy, not because she can't manage on her own."

William stilled. There was truth in that, more than he

wanted to admit. But it wasn't the complete story. "There's something else," he said after a long moment. "I already asked her to marry me. She turned me down."

Roger clearly hadn't expected that. His mouth opened, then closed again. Finally, he found his voice. "When?"

"A few days ago. Right before the poisoning started."

"Did she say why she wouldn't marry you?"

"No. Not really." His gaze drifted toward the distant stretch of range where he'd made the offer. He remembered what he'd said. That they didn't love each other. The words had been practical. Honest. Or so he'd thought.

But then came that kiss two days ago. The way she'd melted into his arms. The way her lips had answered his with no hesitation, no fear. It hadn't felt practical. It had felt like something beyond that.

Maybe he wasn't always practical.

And maybe, just maybe, he hadn't been entirely honest either. Not with her, and not with himself.

"Good Lord," he breathed, the truth hitting him with the force of a stampede.

Roger said nothing at first. Then, with a knowing laugh, he clapped Sage's rump. "I don't know what epiphany just hit you, my friend, but it's about time." With another laugh, he headed for the house.

William remained behind, frozen in place, marveling at his discovery. He didn't need to *choose* to love Keely. He already loved her. Had loved her long before he'd asked her to marry him. He'd simply been too blind—and too foolish—to see it.

Chapter Twenty-Five

The world lay half-asleep when Keely stepped out the kitchen door. Rangeland stretched wide before her, fading into the gray-blue hush of morning. The sun had yet to rise above the jagged peaks of the Tetons, and the sky wore the muted shades of dawn. Mist drifted low over the pasture, weaving like a ghostly veil where a few horses grazed.

She pulled her shawl tighter around her shoulders, bracing against the bite of the morning chill, and hurried toward the chicken yard. From the corral came the hum of men's voices. She could just make out the shapes of the ranch hands saddling their horses. One of them laughed quietly, and the sound carried in the stillness.

After scattering feed for the chickens, she entered the henhouse. Warmth and the familiar scent of straw wrapped around her as she lifted eggs one by one with careful hands.

Through the open doorway, a sliver of sunlight crested the mountains, casting golden light over the land.

The mist glowed with soft hues of rose and amber. Keely paused to take it in. Surely there was no finer sight in all the world than the Tetons bathed in morning light. Cold though the valley mornings might be, she couldn't imagine ever wanting to be beyond the sight of those mountains again.

A short while later, her apron heavy with eggs, she latched the gate behind her and made her way back toward the house. As usual, Rowdy appeared from the barnyard and trotted to her side, tail wagging.

They were nearly to the back door when it opened and William stepped out. He filled the doorway, broad-shouldered and tall, and for a moment, Keely forgot the cold. Her breath caught in her throat, and she came to a sudden halt, nearly upsetting the eggs nestled in her apron.

"Keely." He smiled. "Good morning."

"Morning to you, sir."

"William. Please."

Her cheeks warmed. That infernal flush again.

"We need to talk," he added, his smile turning thoughtful. "Not now. I've got to ride out with the men. But this afternoon, when I return from the range."

She nodded, unsure what else to do.

He stepped further outside. "If it's all right with you, I'd like you to spend the day with Victoria. She told me how much she appreciated your company yesterday. I already spoke with Mrs. Adler about it."

Again, she nodded, although she was confused by the request.

"Maybe you could join her for a walk. She said she

needs the exercise." His gaze dropped to the dog now pressed against Keely's skirts. "I imagine Rowdy's got a bit of energy to burn as well."

"Sure and that's being the truth of it," she said, managing a faint smile.

"I'll see you this afternoon, then."

For a breathless moment, she thought he might close the space between them, might tip her chin up and kiss her again. But instead, he walked past her without pause. Disappointment and relief tangled in her chest.

'Tis better that he doesn't repeat that kiss. Sure and I know it is. For the both of us.

With a long exhale, she stepped through the back door. "Rowdy, stay," she said softly, and the dog obediently dropped to his haunches. She closed the door behind her, knowing he'd be waiting when she came back out.

Inside the kitchen, Chuck was wiping down the work table, already returned to his post-breakfast ritual. He'd washed, dried, and put away all the dishes, pans, and platters. It was always the same. The man didn't allow disorder to linger in his kitchen for long.

If only her own heart were as organized. If only the ache of not knowing what William wanted to say didn't press so heavy on her chest.

"Are you all right?" Chuck asked, glancing up but not halting his hand.

"Right enough." She stepped toward the sink and carefully began unburdening her apron, placing each egg into the large bowl on the counter.

Chuck let out a thoughtful *hmm* but said no more.

A moment later, Mrs. Adler swept into the kitchen, adjusting the ties of her apron behind her back. "Oh, Keely. There you are."

"I fed the chickens and brought in the eggs."

"Thank you, dear. That's a help." Mrs. Adler's tone gentled. "But I think you should take the rest of the day off. Mr. William mentioned you and Mrs. Bernhardt might take a walk this morning. The weather's fine. It'll do you both good to get out in it."

Keely frowned. What was going on?

And then she heard Victoria's voice echo in her memory. *"You really believe none of us have noticed the way you and William behave around each other?"*

Was it that plain to see? Was her heart laid bare for all the world to observe? Had she truly fallen so deeply in love with him that it was written on her face?

Perhaps William felt something for her. Perhaps he meant to say as much this afternoon. But what would she do then? There were secrets between them. *Her* secrets. How could she claim to love a man and keep the truth from him?

The reverend's sage words returned with haunting clarity. Confession and repentance didn't mean she would escape consequences.

What would the consequences be if she told William the truth? If she told him about her lies, that she had taken what wasn't hers and come to Eden's Gate hiding from what she'd done.

Tears pricked her eyes, unbidden and sharp.

Dear Lord, what will become of me if he ever finds out?

It was early afternoon by the time Keely and Victoria left the ranch complex behind. The sun was high, warming Keely's shoulders through the thin muslin of her dress, making the shawl she'd worn that morning unnecessary.

Beyond the cottonwoods that lined the meandering creek, the land stretched wide and open. The Tetons rose in the distance, sharp and blue-gray against a pale horizon. They looked close enough to touch, but Keely knew better. The mountains lay many miles away.

Still, she couldn't gaze at them without something stirring deep in her chest. A feeling between awe and longing, like the memory of a dream just beyond reach.

Rowdy trotted ahead, tail high, ears pricked. Every rustle in the grass drew his attention. When a jackrabbit burst from a tangle of sage, the young dog gave chase, yipping in wild delight. He vanished into the brush, all legs and excitement. Moments later, he came bounding back, tongue lolling, clearly pleased with himself even though he'd caught nothing.

Keely laughed softly, watching him, then let her gaze drift across the valley again. The bunchgrass shimmered silver-green in the light, bowing beneath an invisible hand. In the far distance—so faint it was more sensed than heard—came the soft, rolling murmur of cattle. Likely from the northern pastures, where William and the cowboys had moved the herd this week.

"Peaceful, isn't it?"

Victoria's voice, after their long silence, startled

Keely. She turned toward her friend, who laughed at her surprise. The sound mingled with the gurgling creek.

"Aye. So peaceful 'tis easy to forget there's been trouble about." She cast another glance toward the north. "Do you suppose all is well with them?"

"Don't worry. William will see it through." Victoria pointed to a stone ledge that jutted out above the creek bank. "Come. Let's sit awhile."

They walked toward it, and Victoria eased herself down, letting her boots dangle above the water. Keely joined her, smoothing her skirt as she settled on the sun-warmed rock.

"Is it hard?" she asked after a moment, her gaze shifting to Victoria's belly. "Carryin' the wee one?"

Victoria chuckled. "It's strange, to be honest. I wouldn't say it's easy, but neither is it hard. It's a joy. Every flutter reminds me there's a life growing inside me. A future. And I find my heart making more room for love each day."

A wistfulness fell over Keely. She shrugged it off and asked quietly, "Are you afraid? Of the birthing?"

Victoria's smile turned soft. "Perhaps a little. But I was there when my nephew was born. I saw the pain, but I also saw the wonder that followed. It's a miracle, really."

Keely thought of the poverty that had gripped her childhood. Of mothers in threadbare clothes, doing what they could to feed too many mouths. Her own mam had done everything possible to provide after Da died, but even then, hunger and cold had visited their home far too often. At eleven, maybe twelve, Keely had made a vow. She would not bring children into the world only to suffer. She didn't want to have to steal or beg in order for them to survive.

Not that her mam ever stole or begged. Mam had been a better person than that. But Keely . . .

"Sure and I'm not thinkin' I'd be a good mother."

Victoria's eyes widened in surprise. "Why, Keely Boyle! Whatever makes you say such a thing?"

"Because 'tis the truth."

"And I say it is not." Victoria emphasized her statement with a sharp nod.

"You would not be understanding."

"Then why don't you help me understand?"

Keely took a deep breath and released it slowly. Then, in the hush that followed, she began to speak. She told Victoria about her da's death, and then four years later her mam's. She shared about her time in an orphanage in Ireland—relatively brief, although it hadn't felt that way —and finally of her somewhat frightening journey to England and eventually to Lincolnshire where she'd found work at Hooke Manor. Victoria listened without interrupting, her expression one of genuine empathy. Keely left out the part about how a penniless orphan came up with the money to pay for her ship's passage from Ireland to England, just as she never spoke of how she'd paid her way to America a dozen years later.

"Only God knows why Mrs. Stevens, the housekeeper at Hooke Manor, gave me work," she said finally. "I was a fright when I turned up at the servant's entrance. Starved near to death. Clothes torn, shoes barely holdin' together."

"I can guess why she hired you, Keely. There's a fire

inside you. A will to survive. Mrs. Stevens must have seen that. The same way I did when we first met."

A fire within?

Maybe. She had fought tooth and nail, through hardship and hunger, against loneliness and fear. She had survived. But not always with grace. Not always with honor. Many of the choices she'd made had been her own. She hadn't asked God what to do, hadn't trusted Him to guide her. She had acted out of desperation. And sometimes, out of defiance.

She wanted to be different now.

She wanted to do better.

Was that enough?

Was it too late?

She looked out over the creek, where the water danced and sparkled beneath the sun. Beside her, Victoria sat quietly, not prying, just present.

Keely wrapped her arms around herself and whispered, almost too softly to hear, "I want to be better. But I don't know if I can be."

Chapter Twenty-Six

William intended to propose to Keely again that afternoon, and this time, he was determined to do it right.

"We need to talk," he'd said to her that morning before riding out with the men.

What had she thought in that moment? When she looked back at him and nodded, had she understood what he meant? Had she been hopeful? Or afraid? Was she waiting for him now?

All day long, he'd rehearsed what he would say. Repeatedly, the words turned through his mind. Especially the part where he would tell her they were already more than friends. That he loved her. That he wanted her in his life, not just today or tomorrow, but always.

As Skunk cantered toward the ranch house, William noticed his palms were damp inside his gloves. Nerves. Like a green lad about to ask a girl for the next dance, worried he'd trip over his boots in front of everyone.

But he wasn't a scared boy. There were no fiddles

playing in a crowded ballroom, no girls in fancy gowns. He was a man. A man who finally knew his own heart. And he knew what he wanted for his future.

He wanted Keely Boyle. Wanted to love her, protect her, build a life with her.

The barnyard came into view, and so did four men gathered near the corral. Their horses stood tied to the fence, with heads low and tails flicking. None of the men were his regular hands or any from Major Hasting's crew, either. Those faces, he knew. These were strangers to him. Likely here in response to the ad he'd placed in the Gibeon Weekly Times. Or maybe they'd come on the whisper of word-of-mouth. Either way, he was glad to see them.

He slowed Skunk to a walk, nudging his hat back with one hand. "Afternoon," he called as he approached.

The men stepped away from the fence, forming a loose line.

"We're lookin' for William Overstreet," one of them said.

"You found him." He swung down from the saddle, boots landing solidly in the dirt.

Two men exchanged glances, as if sizing him up.

"We hear you're hiring," another added.

"I am." William's gaze moved steadily down the line —one man, then the next—until it halted on the fourth. Older than the rest. Maybe mid-forties, with a shaggy beard flecked with gray and deep grooves worn into his forehead.

There was something familiar about him. Without that beard, he would look a lot like—

"Hello, William."

He drew back. "Gill? Pastor Gill?"

"Just Anthony now," the man said, stepping forward with an outstretched hand.

It had been at least a decade since William had seen the man, but the memory of him was clear. Anthony Gill was once the circuit rider who'd preached in Gibeon every four or five weeks. Clean-shaven, buttoned up in a stiff black suit, Bible always in hand. He'd spoken with conviction. Delivered sermons with polish.

William grasped the offered hand and gave it a firm shake. "Didn't expect to see you."

"Looking for work," Anthony said simply. "Same as plenty of others."

"You're not preaching anymore?"

He dropped his hand and stepped back. "No. Not in the way I used to. I found other ways to serve the Lord."

William wondered what had caused the man to make such a change. Of the men who'd led the little church in Gibeon over the years, Anthony Gill hadn't been William's favorite, but he'd never doubted his commitment to the ministry. Then again, he didn't know what Anthony had been through in the past decade.

Clearing his throat, he shifted his stance. "All right. Let's talk about what you can do, and I'll tell you what I need."

He motioned the men toward the shade of nearby trees, where a couple of benches waited. The four men followed, and once they settled, William took a seat across from them.

He looked at the young man nearest him. "Let's start with you. Tell me about yourself."

"Looks like the men are back early." Victoria came to a halt and lifted a hand to shade her eyes.

Keely turned her gaze toward the ranch house. Five horses stood tied to the corral fence and hitching post, an unusual sight for the middle of the afternoon. Especially these days, when the ranch hands were keeping a constant watch over the herd, guarding the cattle both day and night.

Beside her, Rowdy gave a sharp bark, as if he, too, found something strange about this unexpected return.

Victoria resumed walking, her pace a touch quicker. No doubt she hoped Roger had returned as well. Keely lengthened her stride to catch up, and as she did, her eyes caught on the small gathering of men seated beneath the trees near the corral. William was among them, and something fluttered in her chest at the sight of him.

"Those are not Eden's Gate men," Victoria observed.

Rowdy must have come to the same conclusion. With another bark, he bolted forward, galloping toward the newcomers like a child toward a sweetshop window. Keely smiled as he barreled into the group. William reached down and caught the exuberant dog, his hands gentle, his expression amused. Instead of scolding, he laughed.

That sound. She loved that sound. Deep and warm and altogether William.

"Come with me," Victoria said, slipping her arm through Keely's. "I'm curious. Aren't you? Let's find out what's happening."

The men all rose as the women approached, an action Keely didn't miss, though her attention was firmly fixed on William. Was he all right? Had there been more trouble? Who were these men? Why had they come?

But then he smiled at her. Ah, that smile. The one she had started to believe was meant just for her. The one that turned her knees to jelly and made her heart skip its rhythm.

"Gentlemen," he said, "may I introduce Mrs. Bernhardt and Miss Boyle."

The men mumbled polite greetings, a couple removing their hats as they nodded.

"These men are here to apply for work on Eden's Gate," William added, turning to Victoria.

"Oh, that's good news," she answered, tightening her hold on Keely's arm for a moment. "We apologize for the interruption and will leave you to your business. Good afternoon, gentlemen." With a graceful nod, she led Keely toward the house.

Keely glanced back once, just as the men disappeared behind the corner of the house. All day long she'd waited for his return, heart fluttering with anticipation, but it seemed she would have to wait a while longer.

"Four isn't very many," Victoria remarked as they reached the porch steps. She released Keely's arm and ascended slowly. "But it's a start. William's advertisement can't have reached too far yet. Perhaps more will come tomorrow. Or the next day."

Keely nodded faintly, her eyes drifting back to the spot where William had stood only moments before.

He was busy. She understood. Of course, she did. And yet . . .

William had learned to trust his instincts about other people. Over the years, that trust had served him well, particularly when hiring the men who worked on Eden's Gate. He could count on one hand the number of times he'd misjudged a man, and even then, he'd recognized the signs early enough to set things right.

As he led the newest group of ranch hands toward the bunkhouse, he found himself cautiously hopeful. Three of the four gave him a good feeling. Solid men, if first impressions meant anything. The fourth? Well, the jury was still out about Anthony Gill. He had no idea why.

William pushed open the bunkhouse door and stepped inside. The room held the familiar scent of pine boards, worn leather, and old coffee grounds. He showed the men where they should stow their gear, which bunks they could use, and where they would eat meals at the long wooden table under the windows.

"My foreman, Jake Foster, will be back soon. He'll give out assignments for the morning." He motioned to the open doorway. "You can put your horses in the corral just there." He paused, giving each man a final once-over. "I'll leave you to settle in."

He stepped out into the sunlight, the warmth hitting his shoulders. He hadn't gone far before a voice called after him.

"William."

He turned to find Anthony standing just outside the bunkhouse, hat in hand, his expression unreadable.

"I wanted to thank you," the former preacher said. "For taking me on. I know it's unexpected and maybe you think it isn't a good change. I appreciate you giving me a chance."

William met the man's gaze without flinching, realizing that's exactly what he'd wondered about. Why did a man answer a call to the ministry and then leave it? But unless Anthony wanted to tell him, it wasn't his business. So he gave a small nod of acknowledgment before turning and walking on.

Chapter Twenty-Seven

Keely lit the lamp on the small table, its glow casting a warm pool of light across the parlor of the cottage. With a quiet sigh, she sank onto the edge of the sofa. Across the room, Rowdy's nails clicked against the floorboards as he trotted toward her. The young dog sat at her feet and gently placed a paw on her knee, his dark eyes full of silent understanding.

Abandoned. Alone. Unwanted. Those were the feelings pressing against her chest.

She leaned forward until her forehead rested against his. "Sure and you do understand, don't you, boyo?"

Rowdy gave a low, mournful whimper.

Keely sat back slowly, brushing a hand through his thick fur before drawing in a steadying breath. It felt as though a thousand hours had passed since she'd stood near the back door of the main house, apron full of eggs, William standing before her with that unreadable look in his eyes.

"We need to talk," he'd said. "This afternoon," he'd promised.

But the afternoon had come and gone. She'd watched as the ranch hands returned from the range, their tired horses unsaddled, others mounted and heading out again with dust rising in their wake. The light had faded, chores had shifted, and shadows had stretched long across the yard. The sun had finally set, leaving her in the cottage's hush with only Rowdy for company.

She loved the dog—had from the start—but he wasn't the one she'd been waiting for. Not all day.

Blinking hard, she pressed her fingertips to the corners of her eyes. She wouldn't cry. Not now. Likely she'd misread William's words, heard more hope in them than he ever intended to give. Perhaps he only meant to apologize for kissing her, for stepping across a line he regretted. Or worse still, perhaps he meant to tell her it was time she left Eden's Gate altogether.

Rowdy rose and turned toward the door.

Keely held her breath.

A heartbeat later, a knock sounded. Just one, firm and clear.

Rowdy barked, the sound echoing like thunder in the small room.

Keely stood, hands trembling slightly as she reached for the knob. William stood on the other side, tall and solid, as if he'd stepped straight out of her prayers.

"Good evening, Keely."

She swallowed hard, her throat tight with emotion. "William." His name escaped in a whisper, barely more than breath.

"I'm sorry it's so late," he said.

"'Tis not so very late."

He smiled. Faint, a little weary. It didn't quite reach his eyes. There was gravity in his gaze, something quiet and unspoken.

"Would you like to come in?" she asked.

"It's better that I don't."

Her heart gave a painful little twist, hope and fear tangling together in fresh confusion.

"Keely . . ." He paused, then cleared his throat. "Keely, I've thought a great deal about what I said the other day. About us. About how we didn't love each other and how friendship might be enough."

She stood motionless, barely breathing, her hands clasped tightly in front of her.

"I realized I was wrong." His voice was softer now, gentled by something deep. "We *are* friends already. But it's more than that." His gaze dropped to Rowdy, who now sat at her feet. "Keely, I don't think you should work for me any longer."

She gasped, a small wounded sound escaping her before she could stop it.

"No," he said quickly, lifting his eyes to hers again, his voice urgent. "Not for the reason you're thinking. I'm not sending you away. What I mean is . . ." He took a deep breath. "Keely Boyle, I love you. And I want to marry you."

The world tilted.

Air thinned.

For one wild moment she feared she might faint, just as she had on her second day on the ranch. Perhaps he saw it too, because he stepped over the threshold, placing both hands on her arms to steady her.

"I love you," he said again, his voice a steady anchor in the swirling storm of her thoughts.

"You love me?" she whispered, scarcely able to believe the words.

"Yes." His smile bloomed. Wide, unguarded, full of light. "I do."

She blinked up at him, dazed. "And why would you be doin' that, I wonder?"

He chuckled softly, the sound like warmth on a winter wind. "So many reasons, Keely. I love how you work without complaint, how you speak your mind no matter who's listening, and I love your honesty. Your questions. Your strength."

"Me honesty?" she whispered. The words echoed in her chest, heavy and sharp, and shame roared to life.

His brow furrowed, as though he sensed something in her silence, but he pressed on. "Do you think you could learn to love me too?"

Tears rose unbidden, stinging her eyes for the second time that night. But she knew her answer. Had known it for days, deep in her soul. "I would not need to learn, William Overstreet. For 'tis true I love you already."

A sound escaped him, one filled with wonder, as he drew her into his arms. His kiss was sweet and slow, gentle and reverent. Not like the fiery, desperate kiss they'd shared a few days ago. This one was different.

This one was a promise.

When he pulled back, she almost reached for him again, unwilling to let go of the moment.

"I'll tell Roger and Victoria," he said, grinning now, joy lighting his face. "And Mrs. Adler, too. They'll help us plan the wedding." He lightly kissed her again, then took a step back. "We'll talk more tomorrow. Goodnight, Keely."

"Goodnight," she whispered, watching as he turned and walked into the darkness, his figure slowly swallowed by the shadows between the cottage and the main house.

She stood in the doorway for a long time, arms wrapped tight around herself, her heart too full for words.

"I love your honesty. Your questions. Your strength." His voice echoed through her memory.

She closed her eyes.

"Sure and I don't have honesty, William," she whispered to the night. "And I don't have courage, for I'm afraid to tell you the whole truth. God have mercy on me poor soul."

William wasn't surprised when Roger appeared in the doorway, his knuckles rapping lightly against the study's doorjamb.

"Figured I'd find you in here," his friend said.

Seated in his chair near the hearth, William set aside the book he hadn't truly been reading and gestured to the opposite chair. "Come on in."

Roger stepped inside and took the seat without hesitation. "You were quiet at dinner."

"I had a lot on my mind."

Roger studied him for a moment. "Thinking about the new men you hired today?"

He shook his head. "No." He hesitated, then spoke the truth. "I was thinking about Keely."

Roger's eyebrows lifted slightly, though his tone remained even. "Ah."

"I told her I didn't need her as a housemaid anymore. I let her go."

"You what?" Roger sat forward, eyebrows arching higher. "You fired her?"

"I had to." He allowed a faint smile. "Because I want her to be my wife instead."

His friend's surprise gave way to a slow, satisfied grin. "You proposed."

"I did."

"And she accepted?"

A quiet laugh rumbled in his chest. "She told me she loves me."

Roger leaned back with a nod of approval. "Victoria thought as much."

"Did she?"

"She did. And, truth be told, I suspected it myself. Funny, isn't it? How a man can look at someone else's life and see love plain as day, yet be blind to what's stirring in his own heart. I nearly missed it with Victoria. Couldn't see the forest for the trees. But here we are."

William nodded, his gaze drifting toward the dark hearth. "I've watched you and Victoria. Amanda and Isaiah. Jocelyn and Sebastian. All of you living lives full of love and purpose. And somewhere along the way, I realized I wanted that too. Something's been missing, and I've found it in Keely."

Roger gave a low chuckle, contentment in his expression. "Good to know you won't die an old bachelor after all."

"Thanks for the vote of confidence," William replied dryly.

Silence settled between them, easy and familiar.

"It's something, isn't it?" he said at last. "That two people from such different worlds—her from Ireland, me from America—could end up in Gibeon at the same time."

"I daresay it's more than something. Sounds like Providence to me."

They sat quietly for a moment longer until Roger leaned forward again.

"You mentioned at supper that you recognized one man you hired."

"I did." William rested an elbow on the chair's arm and ran a hand through his hair. "Anthony Gill. He used to be a circuit rider. Preached here in Gibeon years ago."

"That's quite a change. From preaching sermons to driving cattle."

"My thoughts exactly." William frowned. "He said he's found other ways to serve the Lord. I suppose he meant ministering to cowhands, one soul at a time."

"Does that bother you?"

He let out a slow breath. "I'm not sure. I just can't help wondering *why* he left the ministry. Does it have something to do with integrity? And if so, should I be concerned? I just don't want to unfairly judge him."

"Discernment is a gift, William. Too often people confuse discernment with judgment, but they aren't the same. All I can say is, listen to the Spirit."

He nodded thoughtfully. "You're right. I suppose I'll just have to see how it plays out. Jake plans to pair him with one of our regulars. If he's not pulling his weight—or if something feels off—Jake'll notice."

"Sounds like a good plan."

William's gaze drifted back to the hearth. He didn't want to think about Anthony Gill anymore. Or the long days ahead. Or the reason they'd needed more men.

Not tonight.

Tonight, he wanted his thoughts to linger on gentler things. On Keely's smile. The way her eyes lit up when she laughed. The softness in her voice when she'd told him she loved him too.

A flicker of happiness stirred in his chest, quiet, steady, like the first hint of dawn on the horizon. A new chapter was beginning. For both of them.

He didn't know exactly what lay ahead, but he meant to walk the road with wisdom, one step at a time, with faith as his compass.

For tonight, that was enough.

Tonight, he would let himself look forward to the future.

A future with Keely by his side.

Chapter Twenty-Eight

Keely rose from her bed the next morning feeling as though she hadn't slept a wink. The night had passed in restless silence, her thoughts tangled and relentless. William's words echoed over and over, impossible to forget. Had he truly asked her to marry him? Had he truly said he loved her? Or had she only dreamed it, fashioned a hope so fierce, it had taken on the shape of memory?

She washed and dressed with her usual brisk efficiency, though weariness tugged at her limbs. After taming her unruly curls beneath a white cap, she wrapped a shawl around her shoulders and stepped out into the early gray of dawn.

The barnyard lay still and hushed, painted in quiet shades of silver and blue. Rowdy padded at her heels until she reached for the kitchen door latch. Then, as if grabbed by a mission only he understood, he bounded off into the shadows, tail high, perhaps to rouse the other ranch dogs—the ones that actually worked with the cattle—from their well-earned slumber.

Warmth met her the moment she stepped inside the kitchen. The scent of frying bacon mingled with the familiar clatter of pots and the soft whistle of the kettle on the stove.

"Good morning to you, Mr. Kincaid," she said, slipping off her shawl and reaching for her bibbed apron.

The cook turned, a flicker of surprise crossing his face. "Miss Boyle? What are you doing here?"

Her hands paused mid-motion. "Sure and I'm always here first thing in the morning."

He studied her for a long moment, then slowly crossed his arms over his chest.

And in that instant, she understood. William had told him. Told him she was no longer in service here. No longer a housemaid. Her apron sagged in her hands.

It was all well and good, wasn't it? She loved William. She cherished the thought of being his fiancée. But what would she do with herself all day if not scrubbing floors, dusting bookshelves, or laundering linens? She didn't know how to be idle. Leisure was for women who'd been raised to it. She could stroll the grounds with Victoria, yes, but not forever. And surely William wouldn't want—

The door to the dining room swung open, interrupting her thoughts. And there he was. William.

His smile, when it found her, scattered every worry. "Morning, Keely."

She answered softly, "Morning, William."

Chuck gave a low chuckle and turned back to the

stove, as though the matter was settled by that exchange alone.

"Did you sleep well?" William asked, stepping closer.

She shook her head.

His smile widened. "Neither did I."

Warmth stirred in her belly, slow and sweet.

"You'll eat with us this morning," he said. "Me, Roger, and Victoria."

The words caught her off guard. She parted her lips, ready to object. After her first day at Eden's Gate, she'd eaten every other meal in the kitchen. To sit in the dining room now, even after last night, felt like overstepping. But wasn't this the expected outcome? Not a servant in someone else's home, but the mistress. The woman at William's side.

"Keely?"

She took a breath, pulled from her thoughts.

"You'll eat with us," he said again, his tone gentle.

"Aye, I'll eat with you. But first, I need to see to the chickens and gather the eggs."

"You don't have—"

She lifted her chin. Not defiant, but sure. "Will you be sitting idle this morning, just because you're the master of this ranch?"

He hesitated. "Well, no. But—"

"Then I'll do the work that's mine to do."

In three long strides, he crossed the kitchen and reached for the apron she'd just set down. Without a word, he handed it to her, then stepped behind her and tied the strings at her waist. She felt the warmth of his hands through her dress and almost groaned with the wanting that rose inside of her. He couldn't kiss her—not with Chuck present—but the way his eyes lingered when he turned her to face him felt like the promise of a kiss.

"I'll see you again soon," he said softly, his breath brushing her ear. Then he was gone, vanishing through the dining room doorway as quickly as he'd come.

Keely stood for a long moment, smiling like a fool, unable to help herself. Her heart fluttered with wonder.

Thank You, Father. Thank You for Your mercy and grace. Sure and I can't believe this is happening to me.

With her shawl tucked close around her shoulders, she stepped back out into the morning chill. A chill that couldn't touch the warmth blooming inside her. She had almost reached the coop when a prickle of awareness stopped her mid-step. She turned, scanning the shadows near the barn.

A man stood there—tall, still, half-hidden where light and dark blurred together. Her brow furrowed. One of the new hands William had hired? Or someone else?

"Good morning," she called, lifting her hand in greeting.

He answered with a single word. "Morning." Then he turned and disappeared around the corner of the barn, leaving her staring after him, a strange unease blooming in her chest.

Nerves twisted in William's belly as he stepped out of his study and into the hallway.

Or perhaps he was simply hungry. Yes, that had to be it. Hunger made far more sense than the notion that he might be anxious about sitting down to breakfast with the woman he'd asked to marry him.

Only, it didn't. Not really.

He heard voices drifting from the dining room and followed the sound to the end of the corridor, his footsteps quieter than usual on the polished floor. As he rounded the corner, the sight that greeted him filled him with both relief and a peculiar tightness in his chest.

They had already gathered. Roger sat near the window, posture relaxed. Beside him, Victoria leaned in slightly toward Keely, who sat with her profile toward the entrance. Her apron and cap were gone, and her coppery-red curls framed her face in a soft, untamed halo. Sunlight spilled through the glass panes behind her, catching threads of gold in her hair and casting a warm glow across her features.

She looked up as though she'd sensed him there.

He paused, simply taking her in. If he'd harbored any lingering doubts—he hadn't—they would have vanished then and there. He hoped their children would inherit those wild curls. Her laugh. Her gentle but fierce heart. He'd never pictured children before with any real clarity, but now the thought took root.

"There he is," Roger said with a grin, jolting him back to the moment.

Keely's eyes met his, and he caught a flicker of something. Understanding, perhaps. Or shared imagining.

Her cheeks colored quickly, as though she'd been caught in a thought not so different from his own.

William crossed to the table and pulled out the chair opposite her. "Good morning. Again."

"Good morning," Keely replied, her voice light but quiet.

"It's about time you joined us," Victoria said with a teasing smile. "We were thinking you'd lost your appetite."

He reached for the coffeepot and poured himself a cup, grateful for something to do with his hands. "Had a few things to tend to in my study."

"Well, now that everyone's here . . ." Roger leaned forward, his eyes gleaming with mischief. "When's the wedding?"

Keely startled slightly, and William nearly dropped his cup.

Victoria laughed. "You can't fault us for wondering."

Keely glanced toward him. "We . . . We haven't talked about that part yet."

"No, we haven't. But I reckon we ought to." Especially since he already imagined a future with little people who looked an awful lot like relations to them both.

"Sooner rather than later," Victoria added. "Preferably before our baby comes at the end of August. You'll need to decide what sort of ceremony you want. Will you marry here in the parlor or go into Gibeon for a church wedding? A simple gown or something more elaborate?"

Roger groaned theatrically. "I suppose you'll want me to paint a portrait of the bride. That will take time, I daresay."

Keely laughed. "A portrait? Of me?"

Her tone made it clear she thought the idea outrageous, but William disagreed. A portrait was exactly what he wanted, although not in lace and satin. No, he pictured her out on the open range, the Tetons behind her, the wind in her hair and skirt, strength in her stance.

"What say you, William?" Roger prompted.

"That'd be great," he answered, "but I've a few ideas of my own. I'll tell you later." He turned back to Keely. "In the meantime, you'll be needing those riding lessons we talked about."

"Riding lessons?" A flicker of doubt passed through her eyes.

"You can't always walk or take the buggy. Not out here."

"I'll be supposin' you're right about that."

Roger gestured toward the window. "And I'll bring my sketchbook to capture your first attempts. For posterity, of course."

"Sure but I always thought you a kind man, Mr. Bernhardt. Will you be proving me wrong by what you draw?"

"Perish the thought."

Laughter warmed the room.

William listened to the gentle teasing, his gaze lingering on Keely as her smile lit the space between them. This. This was how life was meant to feel. Like sunlight and promise. Like quiet wonder and something new. Something enduring.

Something worth waiting for.

But not waiting too long, he hoped.

Chapter Twenty-Nine

Several hours had passed since William, Roger, and the ranch hands rode out from the barnyard, but a gentle glow still lingered in Keely's heart. She couldn't remember ever feeling so welcome, so completely a part of something. This morning around the breakfast table had been a revelation. Laughter shared over coffee, the easy teasing between men who respected one another, and the unmistakable warmth in William's eyes whenever they met hers.

More than once, she'd wondered if she might wake to find it had all been a dream. Surely something so good couldn't be real. To keep her feet grounded, she'd turned to work, something solid, something she could see and touch. And what better task than beating the dust from the heavy parlor rug that had needed attention since her arrival?

She and Mrs. Adler had just draped the rug over a sturdy, low-hanging tree branch when the quiet rhythm of the day was interrupted by the creak of wagon wheels.

A buggy rounded the barn and came to a stop, raising a small puff of dust. A moment later, Reverend Truman Blankenship stepped down from the seat.

"Mrs. Adler," he said, lifting a hand in greeting. "Miss Boyle."

The housekeeper gave a polite nod. "Reverend. This is a pleasant surprise."

"I told Miss Boyle at the church potluck I'd pay her a call this week." His gaze shifted toward Keely. "I didn't mean for so many days to pass before I got here. My apologies."

Truth be told, Keely had forgotten the promise entirely. So much had happened in the days since last Sunday afternoon. More than the reverend could guess.

She glanced toward Mrs. Adler, seeking permission. When it came with a nod, she leaned the rug beater against the tree and brushed her hands on her apron before stepping forward. "You're just in time for a bit of quiet, Reverend. The porch makes a fine place to sit, and the breeze is behavin' kindly today."

He smiled. "It certainly is."

Falling into step beside her, Truman folded his hands behind his back. Keely sensed the weight of unspoken words gathering between them. His remark at the potluck echoed in her mind: *It seems to me you have some questions that would be better discussed in a quieter place than this.* She'd forgotten that, too.

Behind them, the soft click of the kitchen door closing signaled Mrs. Adler's retreat, leaving the two of them to their conversation.

As Keely led the way to the porch chairs, she glanced

at her guest. "Would you care for something to drink, Reverend? Some tea, maybe, or coffee?"

"Perhaps before I go. I'm fine for now, thank you." He waited for her to sit first, then settled into the chair beside her, his hands resting lightly on his knees. For a few moments, he simply looked toward the mountains, their deep purples softened by distance and midday light. A slow sigh escaped him. One that spoke of contentment, perhaps even awe. "This is truly a beautiful place."

"Aye," Keely agreed softly, her eyes following his. "It is that."

A quietness fell between them. Not uncomfortable, even though lengthy. At last, the reverend turned toward her, his expression open and kind. "As I recall, you asked me about sin, God's grace, and consequences. Is that right?"

Keely nodded, her gaze dropping to her folded hands.

"Your sin?" His voice was calm, the question posed with gentle patience.

She hesitated. Then gave the faintest whisper. "Aye."

Truman nodded thoughtfully. "First John tells us, 'If we confess our sins, he is faithful and just to forgive us our sins, and to cleanse us from all unrighteousness. If we say that we have not sinned, we make him a liar, and his word is not in us.'"

Her brow furrowed, confusion flickering in her eyes. "God can be a liar?"

"No, no." He leaned forward slightly, shaking his head. "That wasn't clear. I'm sorry. The Scriptures say God cannot lie. But when we deny our own sin, it's as though we accuse Him of being untruthful. That's what the verse means. It's not God who lies. It's we who deceive ourselves."

'Tis me who's the liar, she thought. Those words trembled on her tongue but refused to form. Her throat tightened, shame settling over her like a heavy shawl. Why had she agreed to this visit? She didn't want to talk about her past. Not now, when her heart still held the glow of this morning's joy. Not when she was starting to believe she might truly belong.

"May I tell you something, Miss Boyle?" He hesitated only a breath before continuing. "Conviction is a good and healthy emotion. It's meant to turn us back to God, to bring us to the confession of our wrong-doing. Shame is different. It is a tool of the enemy, used to make us run away from God, to try to hide from Him. The same way that Adam and Eve tried to hide from Him in the garden. I would encourage you to run *to* God, Miss Boyle, not away from Him. Remember always that there is therefore now no condemnation to them which are in Christ Jesus."

She tried to swallow the lump in her throat.

"I'm a good listener." Truman's voice was low, steady. "I've heard the confessions of more souls than you might think, and I promise you, very little surprises me. Whatever it is, you don't have to carry it alone."

"Keely, I—"

The voice came from the doorway, drawing both of their gazes to the front of the house.

Victoria stood just outside, one hand resting on the doorframe. Her brows lifted in surprise before her expression brightened. "Reverend Blankenship! I didn't know you were here. Have you come to help plan Keely and William's wedding?"

"Wedding?" Truman echoed, turning toward Keely in visible confusion.

"We're all so very excited." Victoria breezed across the porch with all the grace of a hostess determined to include everyone in her joy. She lowered herself into the empty chair.

Keely sat motionless, her thoughts scattering. Her mind went blank, and her heart thudded.

Oblivious to Keely's tension, Victoria pressed on. "Roger and I think the wedding should be on Independence Day. Wouldn't that be a delight? Fireworks and bunting, a celebration every year. And if Gibeon continues to grow, perhaps even a parade someday! The whole town celebrating your anniversary, even when you are old and gray." She clasped her hands to her chest. "That gives us over five weeks to plan and make the wedding dress. More than enough time."

The reverend's confusion gave way to polite composure. "A wedding." He nodded slowly. "Well, that is wonderful news. I'm pleased for you both. I will offer William my congratulations the next time I see him."

Whatever Keely might have confessed before Victoria's interruption, the moment had passed. She saw it in the reverend's eyes. A quiet understanding, the resignation of a conversation left unfinished.

She rose, smoothing her apron with trembling hands. "I'll be seein' about your tea now, Reverend. You'll be wantin' something before the ride back to town."

"Thank you, Miss Boyle. I appreciate it."

With a small nod, she walked inside, her thoughts swirling with everything left unsaid.

The sun was high in a cloudless blue sky, and the air was still, save for the occasional buzz of a cicada. Under the meager shade of a cottonwood, the three riders had taken shelter. Their horses stood tethered nearby, heads lowered to graze.

Jake Foster let out a low whistle as he unwrapped a biscuit from oilcloth. He tore off a piece and popped it into his mouth. "Not bad for day-old bread. Of course, I'd trade it for one of Chuck's meat pies any day."

"Wouldn't we all." William bit into a strip of dried beef, chewing slowly, his gaze fixed somewhere in the middle distance. His thoughts had long since wandered back to the ranch house.

Jake eyed him. "You're not thinkin' about meat pies, boss."

He chuckled. "You're right. I'm not."

"Miss Boyle?"

That brought out a grin. "Miss Boyle."

Sitting a little apart from them, Anthony Gill hadn't touched his lunch. "You got a claim to her?"

Jake looked up. "Didn't you hear? Boss here's engaged."

Anthony's hand stilled as he reached for the canteen at his side. "Engaged," he repeated, his voice flat. "To Miss Boyle?"

William nodded, not quite smiling, but not hesitant either. "Yes. We made it official yesterday. Though I reckon it was settled in both our hearts long before that."

Jake gave a satisfied hum. "A good match, if you ask me. I took a likin' to her the first time I saw her."

Anthony lifted the canteen and took a long drink before screwing the cap back on with deliberate care. "I always figured you'd end up with that widow woman in Gibeon. That pretty one. Hannah Gleason, I think her name was."

William blinked at the unexpected name. "Hannah Gleason? I remember her. Sweet-natured, quiet, kind. But I never courted her."

"No?" Anthony's lips twitched. Not quite a smile but close enough. "She spoke well of you. I remember that much."

"I'm glad if she spoke well of me. But that's all there was. She married and moved to Boise City years ago. Six, maybe more. I doubt I've crossed her mind since."

Anthony gave a grunt and tore off a piece of biscuit, chewing it slowly. "Funny how things turn out."

Jake leaned back on his elbows. "Well, not all of us are lucky in love, but at least we're eatin' in good company, eh?"

William nodded, though his eyes slid toward Anthony. The man was looking out at the horizon now, his expression unreadable, his features tight. Something about him didn't sit right with William. "Eating in good company and doing work I love," he said, returning his focus to Jake. "The Lord's been good to me."

Anthony took another slow swig from his canteen

and added, "Especially when it comes to marrying Keely Boyle, I reckon."

William's jaw tightened, his smile fading. He agreed. Marrying Keely would be a blessing. But for some reason, he didn't enjoy hearing Anthony Gill say it.

He didn't like it one bit.

Chapter Thirty

The next two weeks passed in a blur.

Each morning, Keely awoke with the same incredulous thought looping through her mind: *Is this truly happening to me?* And each night, before sleep pulled her under, she whispered a prayer, telling the Lord she didn't deserve to be this happy and thanking Him anyway, from the depths of her heart, for the mercy He'd shown her.

But the world around her hadn't slowed to match the wonder blooming in her soul.

News of another poisoning—this time at the Sanders Ranch—had stirred the sheriff into action. The threat could no longer be dismissed as something that concerned only Eden's Gate. Cattlemen across the region were uneasy now. Wariness hummed like a taut wire beneath every conversation.

While William, Roger, and the ranch hands took shifts guarding the herds day and night, Keely found herself swept into a flurry of wedding preparations. One filled with measurements, fabric swatches, and a hundred other details. The ceremony was set for Sunday, July Fourth—just as the Bernhardts wished—and there was much to do. Victoria and Mrs. Adler made certain no moment went to waste.

Their first order of business had been a trip into Gibeon, where Nancy Davidson, the town's most gifted seamstress, had taken Keely's measurements and assured her she'd begin on the gown straightaway. The dress would be simple, Nancy promised, but elegant. Nothing fussy. Something to suit the bride.

Chuck, not to be left out, declared he would bake a tiered cake to rival the one made for Prince Leopold's wedding. Whether he jested, no one could say for sure. But the gleam in his eye and the scribbled notes on the kitchen worktable suggested he meant it.

Keely often felt as though she'd been caught up in a whirlwind. Part joy, part disbelief, part mounting apprehension.

That same tangle of feelings, combined with the late June heat that lingered indoors, drove her from bed one night. She lit the lamp on her bedside table, slipped into a thin cotton robe, and stepped out into the quiet.

She lowered herself onto the bench outside the cottage door, drawing the robe tighter around her as a faint breeze stirred the air, brushing her skin with a half-forgotten promise of coolness. Leaning back against the cottage's stone wall, she gazed toward the main house. Not a single window glowed. The grand structure lay hushed and dark, swallowed by shadows.

Still, her eyes lifted to the window she knew to be

William's. In just over three weeks, it would be her room too.

A small shiver ran through her, though the night air remained warm.

You must tell him.

The words pressed against her, close as breath. Her conscience again, persistent and unwavering.

You must return what you took. Tell what you did.

She closed her eyes against the insistent thought. The truth, ever present, lay heavy in her chest. It wasn't the gown fittings or the flurry of reception plans keeping her awake. Not even the kisses, although heaven help her, those left her dizzy. No, it was the knowledge that he had said "I love you," that he'd promised forever without knowing the whole truth.

She had let it go on too long. Let him believe in a version of her she'd never corrected.

Tomorrow, she promised herself. *I'll go to him tomorrow.*

A scent interrupted her thoughts—sharp and unmistakable. Cigarette smoke.

Her eyes snapped open.

To the right, near the corral, a faint orange glow pulsed in the dark. "Evening, Miss Boyle," came a voice from the shadows.

Rowdy, who had settled beside her, let out a low growl and pressed against her leg.

"It's me. Anthony Gill."

Her heart thudded. How had he seen her in the dark? Then she realized. Light bled through the curtained window behind her.

"Couldn't sleep?" he asked, walking toward her, the glow of the cigarette tracing his movements.

She tightened her robe, hand brushing over the sash. Her other hand came to rest on Rowdy's head. The dog remained still, but alert.

"I was hoping to find you alone," he continued, stopping short of the lamplight.

That made her shiver again.

"I brought you something. A wedding gift, you might say."

Some of the tension eased from her shoulders. "That's kind of you, Mr. Gill, but it's unnecessary."

"Oh, it isn't much. Picked it up in Jackson Hole. A trader there claimed it was real English tea. When I heard you and William were to be married, I remembered it and figured you, coming here from England and all, might appreciate it." He stepped forward into the light just enough for her to see the muslin packet in his hand. "Please. Take it. I'm no tea drinker. Don't know why I bought it, really. Must've been meant for you from the start."

It would be rude to refuse, wouldn't it? She lifted her hand, palm up. He placed the packet in it.

"Thank you," she said, her voice barely more than a breath.

"Like I said. It's not much. But I wish you and William all the happiness you deserve." He flicked the cigarette to the ground and crushed it beneath his boot heel. Then he turned and walked away, vanishing once more into the shadows.

Keely sat unmoving. The little pouch of tea rested in

her lap, the faint scent of smoke still hanging in the air. Rowdy hadn't relaxed, not entirely. He pressed close, muscles taut.

The night had cooled, but the unease in her chest remained.

Tomorrow, she told herself again. *Tomorrow, I will tell William the truth.*

No more waiting.

No more silence.

Tomorrow.

Chapter Thirty-One

id a man have any right to feel as happy as
William did? Especially when someone—
some misguided soul with a heart full of
malice—was roaming the countryside, poisoning cattle
without rhyme or reason. There were real dangers in the
world. Sorrows. Injustices. And yet, there he was,
standing at the center of his own joy, thinking only of
himself and the woman he was soon to marry.

In the stillness before dawn, he descended the stairs
and made his way to his study. The house was silent
around him, save for the soft creak of the floorboards
underfoot. He lit the lamp on his desk, the warm glow
pushing back the gray edges of morning, then sank into
his favorite chair. He opened his Bible and rested it across
his lap, hoping the familiar words would ground him.
But this morning, they slipped through his mind like
mist.

He tried to fix his thoughts on truth, on grace, on
mercy, but they refused to stay tethered. Again and again,

they wandered, always back to the young Irish maid asleep in the cottage across the barnyard.

Keely.

That wild tumble of red hair.

The spark in her green eyes, always quick and bright.

The way a blush could bloom so suddenly in her cheeks, flaring warm as candlelight.

He gave a quiet huff of laughter. It seemed foolish now that he hadn't recognized it sooner, all that she meant to him. He couldn't even trace the moment it had begun. Perhaps it was the day she'd first arrived at Eden's Gate, tired, bewildered, with eyes too wary for someone her age. Or perhaps it had been the next day, when she had fainted dead away in his parlor. A grin tugged at the corners of his mouth at the memory. Should he have felt a pang of jealousy that she'd come seeking Roger and even swooned at the sight of him? Possibly. But it hardly mattered now.

She loved him. She wanted to be his wife. That truth still left him stunned, a little breathless. And deeply grateful.

He exhaled slowly and closed the Bible, bowing his head.

Lord, forgive me, but I am far too elated to think on anything or anyone but the object of my affections.

A soft chuckle escaped him as he rose. If he couldn't settle his heart with Scripture, he might as well turn his attention to something more practical. Figures and columns awaited. Tedious perhaps, but necessary. Numbers wouldn't stir up dreams or distractions.

Crossing behind his desk, he reached for the ledgers

and pulled one down from the shelf. The binding creaked slightly as he opened it. Accounts needed tending, and maybe—just maybe—they could hold his focus.

Surprisingly, they did. At least for a little while.

He was halfway through reconciling livestock expenditures when a light rap on the doorframe drew his eyes up from the page.

Mrs. Adler stood there, arms folded, eyebrows arched with practiced authority. "It's near time for breakfast, Mr. William, and you've yet to pour your first cup of coffee."

He glanced toward the window. Pale morning light now spilled freely across the study floor, golden and soft. "I lost track of time."

She stepped forward and extended an envelope. "This turned up in Logan's saddlebag. Must've missed it when he brought in the rest of the post yesterday."

He accepted it with a smile, recognizing Jocelyn's neat, unmistakable hand at once. The monogram on the flap—J.C.W., Jocelyn, Countess of Hooke—still gave him pause, even after nearly two years.

He ran his thumb underneath the wax seal.

"I'll leave you to your letter," Mrs. Adler said, satisfaction in her tone as she turned and left the room.

William sat down again, smoothing the paper and beginning to read.

Hooke Manor
Lincolnshire
20 May 1897

Dearest William,

We hope this letter finds you in good health. I often picture Eden's Gate in springtime, when the wildflowers begin to blanket the range. It makes me smile to imagine you on horseback, riding through that sea of purples, whites, and golds.

Sebastian continues to thrive in his role as earl and is certainly one of the most beloved masters ever to reign at Hooke Manor. He enjoys working with the tenants, and they admire and appreciate him. Of course, he and Adam have increasing hopes that one of their horses will win the Grand National one day. You should see them, assessing mares and studs, talking over prospects late into the night.

Little Edward sends love to his Uncle William. He is very close to walking, and his babbling even begins to make sense to me. I think it won't be long before he is talking. Can you believe it? And though I hardly dare put it to paper, we hope to give Edward a sister come Christmastime. But if it should be a brother, we will rejoice just as much.

I was surprised to hear you've hired a maid. I can hardly imagine Mrs. Adler allowing another woman into her realm. She's been so particular since Mother passed. But what astonished me most was to learn the maid is Keely Boyle. I remember her as quiet and capable, excellent at what she does, though we never exchanged more than a few polite words.

It is with some reluctance that I write this to you now, but I feel compelled to do so, as the matter touches your household. Some time ago, I discovered that a sum of money was missing from my sitting room, along with several pieces of Whitcombe family jewelry and, most distressing of all, our mother's brooch. You may recall it. Gold, in the shape of a forget-me-not, engraved with Mother's initials, C.M.O. Though its value is only sentimental, I had long intended to pass it on to a daughter one day.

We kept the matter quiet at first, not wishing to cast suspicion without cause. But just recently, one of the undermaids came forward. She remembered seeing Keely near the cabinet where the money and jewelry were kept. This was the day before Keely's abrupt departure. Regretfully, I believe we now have sufficient reason to suspect she took the money and jewelry.

I do not share this to distress you, only so that you may be aware. The thought grieves me deeply. I cannot say what desperation might have driven her to such an act. Still, the loss stings. I trust both wisdom and grace will guide you in deciding how best to proceed.

I remain your affectionate sister,
Jocelyn

William inhaled sharply, only then realizing he'd been holding his breath.

Keely? A thief?

No.

No, he couldn't believe it. Wouldn't believe it.

His gaze slid to the mantel, to the three keepsakes arranged there, and in particular, the stone in the middle. He remembered wondering, when it disappeared, if Keely had taken it. He'd quickly dismissed the idea, especially after the stone reappeared without anyone saying a word. It hadn't seemed all that important.

But a skipping stone was one thing. Money and family jewels were something else entirely.

He rose from his chair in a single swift motion and crossed the room. Hand reaching for the latch, he didn't pause to consider what he would say. Only that he had to see Keely.

Now.

Keely opened the top drawer of the old maple bureau, the wood creaking faintly in protest. Her fingers reached for the linen handkerchief tucked deep in the corner, hidden beneath a folded petticoat. Nestled inside was Lady Hooke's brooch. She unwrapped it carefully, the gold forget-me-not gleaming dully in the dim morning light.

If only she'd never taken it. If only she hadn't let desperation and fear guide her steps that day. But she had. And this morning, she meant to make it right. She couldn't return the money. Or the jewelry that she'd sold. But she could return this. The one thing she still had. The one thing she couldn't seem to stop thinking about.

She closed her fingers around the brooch, readying herself. And then came a sharp pounding on the cottage door.

She jumped. The brooch slipped in her grasp. Heart thudding, she pressed the pin tightly to her chest and hurried toward the parlor, dread pooling in her stomach.

She opened the door and saw William standing on the other side, his shoulders squared, jaw set.

Her breath caught. "William? What is it? Has something happened?"

"I need to speak with you." He held up a folded letter in one hand. His eyes searched hers. "I've had word from Jocelyn. I need to know if what she suspects is true."

"Lady Hooke?" The name barely made it past her lips. Her spine stiffened, a tremor passing through her.

"She wrote about you," he said. "About things that went missing. Money. Jewelry."

The brooch dug into her palm as she clenched her hand tighter. A sudden sting bloomed where the pin pressed into flesh.

"Jocelyn believes you stole from her."

Her vision blurred as tears welled, stinging hot against her lashes.

"Keely, is it true?"

Her throat ached with the effort to speak. She tried to form the words, but they tangled at the edge of her tongue. "I—" She swallowed hard, then tried again. "I . . .

I was going to tell you. Sure and I was coming to tell you now."

His eyes didn't leave hers. "Tell me what?"

Slowly, she opened her hand and held it out to him. The brooch lay in her palm, bright and terrible, its delicate shape as damning as any confession.

"I kept this," she whispered. "I shouldn't have done. I'm ever so sorry, William. Truly, I am. Ever so sorry."

She couldn't say more. Couldn't explain the knot of shame, the long, silent guilt she'd carried across an ocean and through almost every moment since. Her voice failed, but her tears did not.

Hours later, atop a high ridge, William stared down at the herd of cows and calves grazing in the basin below. But he saw none of it. His eyes were open, but his thoughts remained tangled in the memory of this morning, in the image of Keely standing in the cottage's doorway, pale as a ghost, the brooch in her open hand.

"I'm ever so sorry, William. Truly, I am. Ever so sorry."

The words had struck him like a blow. He hadn't answered. Hadn't spoken a single word. Just turned on his heel and strode to the barn. After saddling and bridling Sage, he'd ridden away from the ranch complex, never glancing toward the cottage, never knowing if Keely had stood there still, hoping he would talk to her.

And now the silence between them sat heavier than any conversation might have.

She *had* stolen. Not from a stranger, not even from a neighbor, but from his sister. From Jocelyn. Money and jewelry, including their mother's brooch. Keely had taken them, kept them, and said nothing in all this time. Not until this morning, when the truth finally came out.

He thought he'd known her. Thought he'd seen her clearly.

And yet.

She'd been desperate. Alone. Running from a man who would've done unspeakable harm if she'd stayed. That part of her story had always been clear. He believed her even now. And he would have done anything to help her escape if he'd known her then. Wouldn't he?

"I'm ever so sorry, William. Truly, I am. Ever so sorry." The words echoed again, soft and broken. She hadn't defended herself. Hadn't denied it or tried to explain it away. She had simply looked at him with those wide, grief-stricken eyes and told the truth by what she held in her hand.

He should've listened. Should've stayed. He should have given her a chance to say more. He loved her. This revelation hadn't changed that.

His gaze lifted toward the west. He couldn't see the house from here, couldn't see the barn or the cottage or the corrals, but he knew exactly where they lay. Nestled down below, in the crook of the land he loved. And there, in one of the smallest of those buildings, was Keely.

And he wanted to be there. With her.

He gathered the reins in one hand, ready to nudge Sage forward, when he caught a movement in the corner of his vision. Jake Foster was cantering his horse up the slope, kicking up a thin ribbon of dust behind him.

William waited, settling back into the saddle.

"You left early," Jake said as he reined in. "Did you even take time for breakfast?"

"I had some things to think over."

Jake gave a knowing nod. "Lot goin' on." He hesitated, then added, "Thought you oughta know. Gill cleared out during the night."

William lifted a brow. "Gone?"

"Not a word to anyone. Didn't even wait for his pay."

He wasn't sorry the man was gone. He couldn't say why, but in the two weeks since he hired Anthony, he'd felt a growing distrust. Nothing he could put his finger on, but there all the same.

Jake continued, "We've got enough men now to cover the range. As good as anybody can expect."

"I reckon."

"Well—" Jake turned his horse in the opposite direction. "I'll leave you to your thinkin'." With that, he rode back down the slope.

William watched for a moment longer. But he knew thinking wouldn't fix what troubled him.

He turned Sage toward home.

He had a woman to face—and a future to reclaim.

Chapter Thirty-Two

K eely entered the kitchen, grateful to find it empty. She'd seen Chuck heading toward his quarters not long ago. Victoria was likely in the parlor with a book, and Mrs. Adler could be anywhere in the house, cleaning and fussing with her usual efficiency.

She removed her shawl and laid it over the back of a chair, then crossed to the stove. The familiar sight of the big iron kettle waiting on its trivet brought a small measure of comfort. Tea, she understood. Tea she could control.

She lifted the kettle, sloshed out the cool water inside, and refilled it at the pump. The metal rang softly as she set it back in place. Then she reached for the small muslin bag on the table, the one Anthony Gill had given her late the night before.

"When I heard you and William were to be married, I remembered it and figured you, coming here from England and all, might appreciate it."

She pressed her lips together against the memory. She'd still known happiness when the ranch hand said that to her. But would she ever know it again? William knew the truth now. He knew what she'd done. She'd tried to tell him she was sorry, but he'd walked away without a word. The look on his face may as well have been a blow.

She opened the pouch and poured the contents into her palm. Ordinary tea leaves—dark, fine, fragrant. Nothing remarkable. She fetched the small teapot, rinsed it with warm water, and spooned the leaves inside.

The kettle began to hum and sputter. She poured the boiling water over the leaves, the steam curling up into her face. For one fragile moment, she closed her eyes and breathed in the familiar scent.

Oh, for a cup of tea shared with someone who loved her. For forgiveness freely given. For the chance to start again.

Swallowing back the pain in her heart, she covered the pot with a folded towel to keep in the heat while it steeped, then reached into the cupboard for a china cup and saucer, white with a delicate blue border. One of Mrs. Overstreet's pieces from long ago, most likely. When the tea was ready, she set a small wire strainer over the cup and poured. Amber liquid slipped through the mesh, but the steam carried an odd smell. Medicinal, almost. She added a spoonful of sugar, then wrapped her fingers around the cup and lifted it to her lips.

The taste was wrong. A little bitter. It reminded her of a tonic her mam once made her drink when she was small. She added another scoop of sugar and stirred.

One sip. Then another and another. Still bitter. She added more sugar.

Mr. Gill might have meant well by giving her this bag of tea leaves, but she was thinking whatever he'd paid for it, it had surely been too much. Still, she took more sips of the brew until the cup was nearly empty. Waste not, want not.

She had no idea how long she stood there at the kitchen counter—the near-empty cup in her hand, her thoughts wandering to William, to the brooch, to her sorrow—before the back door banged open, jerking her thoughts to the present.

"Get back, Rowdy." Chuck's voice boomed through the kitchen. "Get back before you trip me! Look out now!"

Rowdy barreled inside, tongue lolling, and launched himself toward her.

"Rowdy, no!" she cried.

His paws hit her thighs. The remaining tea splattered onto her blouse.

"Rowdy! Bad boy!"

She turned, reaching for a cloth, when a rolling wave of dizziness slammed into her. The room tilted. The cup slipped from her fingers and shattered on the floor, the sound oddly distant, as though underwater. Her stomach clenched. A bitter, metallic taste flooded her mouth. She grabbed for the edge of the table, but her legs buckled.

Voices blurred. Chuck shouted her name. Rowdy whined, paws skittering on the floorboards.

Keely hit the ground hard, her cheek against the cool wood.

Darkness rushed up to meet her.

And then . . . nothing.

There was no answer to William's knock on the cottage door. The silence only strengthened his resolve. He reached for the knob, intent on finding Keely. His thoughts were consumed with her, with the truth he needed to understand about what had happened in England all those months ago. And more than that, by all the things he'd left unsaid. Things he could no longer keep to himself.

When he didn't find her within, he turned away and crossed the yard toward the main house. He supposed she might be in the kitchen at this hour. He'd start there.

But just as he stepped through the front door, a voice rang from above. Mrs. Adler's, distant and indistinct. At the same moment, he spotted Victoria halfway up the stairs, a porcelain pitcher in her hands.

"Go, man!" Chuck's voice roared from the kitchen. "Now!"

William flinched, unsure who the cook was shouting at. But a slammed door told him someone had already bolted off on an errand. He stepped further inside.

"Victoria?" he called out.

She turned at the landing, worry etched deep across her brow. "William. Thank God you're here. Come quickly." She didn't wait for him to respond, only vanished into a nearby room.

His heart thudded hard and fast. Something was wrong. Dread built with every step as he mounted the stairs two at a time.

Keely's name beat through his mind like a drum. But nothing could have prepared him for what he saw. She lay motionless in the bed, a thin coverlet drawn up to her waist. Her face was pale as milk, drained of the color he loved so well. Her eyelashes were still against her cheeks. Even her breathing, barely perceptible, seemed not quite real.

"Keely?" He dropped to the edge of the bed and reached for her hand, needing to feel its warmth, its weight.

She didn't stir.

His head jerked toward Victoria, then toward Mrs. Adler, who hovered near the door.

"What happened?" he demanded.

Mrs. Adler's face was drawn, her voice uncertain. "We don't rightly know." She stepped forward a little. "She'd made herself a cup of tea. That's all. Then Rowdy came barreling in from the yard. Jumped up on her."

"He knocked her over?"

"No." She shook her head. "The dog didn't knock her down. Mr. Kincaid said she even scolded Rowdy. Same as always. But then she swayed . . . and collapsed."

He looked back at Keely, her hand limp in his. "She fainted," he said, almost to himself. Fainting wasn't so terrible. He'd seen her swoon once before, and she'd recovered within moments.

Victoria stepped closer, a hand settling gently on his

shoulder. "It seems more than a faint. She hasn't moved since Mr. Kincaid laid her on the bed."

Mrs. Adler added softly, "We've sent a rider for the doctor."

His thumb brushed along Keely's icy fingers. "How long has she been like this?"

Neither woman answered. The silence told him more than words. Too long.

"May I get you something?" Mrs. Adler asked gently. "You left before breakfast and—"

"I need nothing." His voice cracked despite the effort to hold it steady. "Thank you."

He bowed his head, forehead nearly touching the back of Keely's hand. It lay limp in his.

All he wanted—all he could think to want—was for her to open her eyes. To smile. To breathe easily again. To say, *Sweet sufferin' cats!* the way she always did when life surprised or exasperated her.

The two women retreated, the door closing with a quiet click behind them. And still he didn't lift his head.

"Keely Boyle," he said after a long while, his voice raw. "I'm here. I'm not leaving. No matter what comes. There are things I need to say. Things you deserve to hear. I think I understand now. What happened in England. Why you did what you did. I should've listened. I should've given you a chance to speak this morning. But I was—" He stopped, jaw clenched. He took a slow breath and continued. "I was angry. I let my pride take root. You need to know this, Keely. I forgive you. Do you hear me? I forgive you. And I hope you'll forgive me." His throat closed. His vision blurred. Tears spilled freely now. "I love you. I'll love you for the rest of my days. So please. Come back. Come back to me, Keely. Let me show you what love looks like when it stays. Let me fight for you."

Still, she didn't move. He pressed her cool hand between both of his, willing his warmth into her still fingers.

"Father in heaven," he whispered, "save her. Please. Whatever this is, whatever brought her to this bed, let it not be the end of her story. Heal her. I beg You. Forgive me for my hard heart, for my failure to listen, for my pride. You are merciful, Lord. Be merciful now."

And in the hush that followed, William stayed. Her hand cradled in his, his prayers lifted one after another, words he would not stop repeating until she answered him at last.

Please, God. Let her answer me at last.

More than two hours later—an eternity in William's mind—Oxford Grant released his hold on Keely's wrist and straightened, his expression unreadable.

"Well, Doctor?" William asked, his voice tight, each word clipped by the tension coiling in his chest. Impatience and dread warred within him, each breath a struggle not to give in to fear.

Dr. Grant didn't answer immediately. Instead, he leaned forward again, fingers brushing lightly across Keely's cheek before lifting one of her eyelids. He watched in silence for a moment, his brow furrowed in concentration.

"There's no fever," he said at last. "Her pulse is quite slow, but it's steady." His tone was calm, deliberate. "Her breathing's shallow. Noticeably so. But no longer to the point of danger."

William didn't move, didn't dare interrupt.

"I'd wager she's been drugged," the doctor went on. "Laudanum perhaps, or one of its cousins. It's possible she was poisoned, but based on what I'm seeing, that seems less likely."

The word poison landed like a stone in William's gut. He gritted his jaw, his body taut, willing himself not to show panic. Someone had poisoned his cows, and they died in agony.

Dr. Grant shook his head slowly. "Whatever the drug, the dose wasn't large enough to kill her. If it had been, she wouldn't be with us now."

William's throat constricted even more.

"She may sleep for several more hours. When she wakes, she'll likely be weak. Disoriented. Possibly nauseated. Barring any unexpected turn—"

"But she'll recover?"

"Yes, I believe she will. I cannot swear it, but experience tells me she will recover." Dr. Grant's gaze was steady as he repeated, "She's going to be all right, William. I'm reasonably confident of that."

Relief hit. Swift, hard, and all-encompassing. He closed his eyes. *Thank You, Jesus. Thank You.*

He dropped to his knees beside the bed, his hands finding hers. Her fingers lay limp in his grasp, as before, but he felt the pulse in her wrist, and it eased the tightness in his chest.

If he had his way, he'd never let go again.

Opening her eyes felt like lifting a mountain. For a moment, Keely let herself drift again, sinking into the soft pull of dreams. Mam humming as she stirred the pot over their small hearth. Da's laugh rolling through the tiny stone cottage tucked into the Irish hills. Warmth. Safety. That dream-world beckoned, urging her to remain in its comfort a little longer.

But something stronger called to her.

A voice.

William.

With effort, she surfaced from the fog. Curtains had been drawn, muting the light and leaving the room cast in soft shadow. This wasn't her cottage. The air smelled different. Lavender and wood polish.

"Keely?"

The sound of his voice came again, close and familiar.

She tried to turn her head, but the world lurched sideways, her stomach roiling. A low groan escaped before she could stop it, and she squeezed her eyes shut against the dizziness.

"Just lie still."

William.

She wasn't dreaming. The certainty brought a fragile comfort to her chest. She wanted to see him—needed to see him—but instinct told her to wait until the spinning stopped.

"I need to tell you something," he said, his mouth close to her ear.

She tried to shape words, but all that emerged was a whispered breath.

"I realized something while I've been waiting for you to wake up."

With great effort, she whispered, "That you love me?"

She received a soft chuckle in reply. "No. That I already knew."

Her heart fluttered at his words. The spinning eased. She opened her eyes slowly, careful not to move her head, and this time the world stayed steady. William sat on the edge of the bed, his form outlined in the dusky light, right where she could see him.

"Hello," he said, a smile tugging gently at his mouth.

"Hello." Her voice was faint. "What happened?"

"You lost consciousness," he said. "For most of the day."

"I . . . fainted?" She almost shook her head but stopped herself in time.

"It was more than that." His smile faded. "Dr. Grant believes you were drugged."

"Drugged?"

"Mrs. Adler thought the tea you made smelled strange so she asked Dr. Grant. He confirmed the leaves had been soaked in laudanum. I guess laudanum has a distinctive scent."

Tea. The memory struck. A strange odor. An odd

bitterness on her tongue. The sugar not helping. Rowdy leaping up. And then darkness. Like a curtain falling.

Her lashes lowered. "I should've told you," she murmured, but the thought slipped away before she could catch it fully.

"Keely?"

"Hm?"

"I'm sorry."

Her brows knit. "You? Why?"

"For this morning. For the way I let my pride take hold of my words. As if I thought I would be above making similar choices to the ones you made. And that isn't true. It's a hard thing to admit."

She stared at him. "You've forgiven me? For what I did?"

"God forgave me. How could I not forgive you?" He took her hand, cradling it gently between both of his. "For everything. The past, and whatever comes after. All of it."

Her throat worked. A confession rose unbidden. "I took the little stone from your study, too. The one on the mantel."

"Why?"

"I'm not thinkin' I know." A small, rueful smile touched her lips. "But I brought it back."

"I know." His thumb brushed over her knuckles. "Why?" he asked again, softer.

"Because it wasn't mine to keep. It meant somethin' to you. I suppose . . ." She swallowed. "I needed you to have it more than I needed to hold on to it meself."

Silence stretched between them, broken only by the

faint rustle of the curtains and the soft sound of Keely's breath.

William's voice dropped to a tender murmur. "You are a mystery, Keely Boyle." His smile deepened. "I mean to spend the next forty or fifty years, God willing, unraveling every bit of that mystery. And I'm going to enjoy every single moment of it, too."

Epilogue

Eden's Gate Ranch
September 1897

The late afternoon sun spilled gold across the shoulders of the Tetons, as if the heavens themselves were bidding farewell to summer. Keely strolled through the paddock, her skirts brushing against long grass gone sun-dry at the tips. Rowdy padded beside her, alert but calm, his gaze fixed on the mares and their late-season foals. He didn't bark or bolt to chase—not even once—which pleased her more than she could say.

"Good boy," she said, reaching down to stroke the top of his head.

She lifted her gaze toward the eastern rise, where the hills gave way to open meadow and pale sky. There he was. William. She could tell it was him long before she saw his face. A wife came to know the way her husband sat a horse, how he carried himself with calm strength and quiet purpose. And even if she hadn't recognized his form, the black stallion was unmistakable.

A smile curved her lips as she moved toward the fence, slipping between the rails, her heart already rushing to meet him. He must have seen her, too. Skunk shifted from a canter into a full gallop, and the way William leaned into the wind made it plain. He was just as eager to reach her as she was to greet him.

They were a good match in every way that mattered.

For a breathless second, she thought he meant to ride straight through her, but she didn't move. She didn't doubt him. Not in the saddle. Not in life. He brought the stallion to a sharp halt just feet from where she stood, dry earth billowing around her boots in a fine cloud.

She coughed once and laughed as the dust swirled past her.

Then he was off the horse and in her arms almost before his boots hit the ground. He pulled her close and held her fast.

"I love seeing you out here waiting for me," he said, his breath warm against her ear.

He kissed her then—long and tender, with the kind of hunger that made her heart leap and her breath catch. When at last he pulled away, she was flushed and grinning, her hands still clinging to the front of his shirt as if she wasn't quite ready to let him go.

He turned to gather Skunk's reins, then slipped his free arm around her waist, tucking her to his side as they began the slow walk toward the barn.

"I have news," she said after a moment, casting him a sideways glance.

"You do?"

Most evenings she had something to share—a story from town, a new recipe tried, another chore mastered, a letter received. She took pleasure in the small things, and so did he. But today's news was different. Today's news would matter.

"You'll want to hear it," she said, nudging him lightly with her shoulder. "Two things, in fact. Both for you."

He smiled. "Well then. I'm listening."

She waited a beat, enjoying the moment. "The sheriff stopped by. Seems Mr. Gill's been arrested. They caught up with him in Salt Lake. Too much whiskey, too little sense, and he started bragging. About what he did to you, to the other ranchers, and to me."

William's smile faded. His jaw tightened.

"He talked loud enough for a deputy to take notice. They wired Idaho Falls and made the connection right away. The sheriff says Gill will face more than a few charges. Apparently Eden's Gate wasn't the only place he's done this, but it will be the last. Sure and he won't be troubling anyone again."

William let out a long breath and shook his head. "Thank God."

"Aye," Keely said quietly. "God be praised."

"Did he happen to say *why* he did it?"

She shook her head.

"I suppose we'll never know." He gave her hand a gentle squeeze. "And the second thing you wanted to tell me?"

"Roger sent word." Her smile returned. "Victoria's had her baby."

He stopped mid-step, turning to face her fully. "What?"

Keely laughed at his expression. "A daughter. She came fast. So fast they couldn't even send for me. Not that I'd have been much help, truth be told."

"A daughter." His face lit with wonder, as if the word itself held magic.

"She's healthy, and so is Victoria. Roger says the babe's got a lusty cry and a good grip." She paused, her voice softening. "He's already wrapped around her wee finger, I'll be thinkin'."

William chuckled. "Poor man never stood a chance."

"Few fathers do," Keely said, sliding her hand into his. "Especially when it's a daughter."

They walked on as the sun sank lower, stretching long shadows across the fields. From the barn came the rustle of hay, the steady creak of leather, the low nicker of horses. The hush of evening had settled over Eden's Gate, broken only by the murmur of wind in the cottonwoods and birdsong in the air.

At the gate, William paused again and turned to face her. "Do you ever think about what we might've missed? If things had gone differently. If you hadn't run from Hooke Manor."

"Sometimes." Keely tilted her head, her eyes thoughtful. "But only for a moment. Then I look around, and I know I was never meant to be anywhere else."

He leaned down and kissed her forehead. "You're my home, Keely. Always."

"And you're mine."

They stood there in the quiet, husband and wife,

hearts still learning the rhythm of a shared life but anchored in grace, tested by truth, and held fast by love.

William dropped the reins and drew Keely into an embrace. This time, his kiss was longer still—thorough and sure and filled with everything words could never quite say.

When he finally pulled back, she looked up at him with a smile and whispered, "Sweet sufferin' cats."

He laughed then, head thrown back, face to the sky.

Oh yes. She had truly found where she belonged. God Himself had seen to that.

Did you enjoy *To Find Where She Belongs*? I hope so! Please take a minute to leave a review. Just a sentence or two sharing what you liked about the book!

https://amzn.to/4jbpmbi

Coming Soon

TO FALL IN LOVE AT CHRISTMAS

Gibeon, Idaho
November 1897

A blast of frigid air greeted Truman Blankenship as he left the parsonage and began walking west along Main Street. Patches of snow clung to the shadowed sides of buildings, reminders of the sudden squall that had blown across the range on the last day of October. If this year's *Old Farmer's Almanac* was correct, they were in for plenty more such storms in the coming months.

"Good morning, Reverend," Harry Hathaway greeted him outside the mercantile. "Wonderful sermon last Sunday."

"Thank you, Harry." He touched the brim of his fur-lined fedora with a gloved finger. "Much obliged." Hunching his shoulders against the cold, he kept moving.

Truman had served as the pastor of Gibeon Chapel for five years now, but the town, its residents, and the church were so familiar to him, it felt as if he'd always lived and served there. Of course, at twenty-seven years old, he was almost as old as the town itself. There were still a handful of members in the congregation who thought him too young to lead them, although fewer now than in the beginning. He'd received the position, he knew, because no one else had applied. It helped somewhat that the people of Gibeon had first known him as a circuit rider. They'd heard him preach and, despite his youth, had liked him.

He stepped off the boardwalk to make room for Nancy Davidson but stepped up again when he saw her drop her key as she tried to insert it in the door to her dress shop. "Let me get that for you, Miss Davidson."

"Oh, thank you, Reverend. My fingers are numb from the cold. Can you believe how quickly the weather changed?"

"Allow me." After picking up the key, he put it in the lock and turned it, then opened the door and dropped the key into Nancy's waiting hand. "Best get inside and start a fire in that stove."

"I will. Thank you."

Once again, he tapped a finger against the brim of his hat, then moved along.

Word had come to him yesterday afternoon that Donny, the youngest Jackson boy, was sick in bed again. The lad had suffered bouts of fever and cough off and on for the past year. His recently widowed mother, Fern Jackson, always looked as if she might fall ill next, if from nothing else than sheer exhaustion. Truman wanted to assist her in whatever way he could, and he would pray for the boy even if she did not want help.

The Jackson thirty-acre farm was less than a quarter mile west of Gibeon. The home was small, the house and outbuildings not in the best of shape. Wes Jackson had always spent more time in the saloon in town than he had caring for his property or his family. A shame, really, because he could have known great pleasure with the wife and sons God gave him.

Truman crested a rise in the road and caught his first glimpse of the farm. The sight confirmed his thoughts of minutes before. One hinge on the gate was missing, and the rest of the fence that bordered the road sagged and weaved, looking as if someone could knock it down with a single breath. The sun, wind, and time itself had faded the boards of the house. Come spring, he promised himself, he would get together some men, and they would whitewash the house and shore up the porch while they were at it.

At the front door, he knocked and waited for an answer, telling him to enter. That's what often happened when he called on members of his congregation. Instead, Nathan opened the door. The boy was thirteen years old and trying hard to be the man of the house.

Truman removed his hat. "Hello, Nathan. I've come to see your mother and brother."

"Ma's seeing to Donny." He widened the opening. "But you can come on in, sir."

"Thank you."

The front parlor was chilly, despite a fire in the wood

stove. The kindling box against the wall was almost empty, and there were only a few split logs next to it. He suspected the Jackson family hadn't been prepared for the cold to arrive so soon. That was an immediate need he could help with.

Nathan moved to the blanket that hung in the opening between the front and back rooms. Moving it aside with one hand, he said, "Ma, Reverend Blankenship is here."

"Bring him back," Fern answered.

Truman stepped forward, holding his hat in his left hand, his Bible in his right.

The bedroom that served Fern Jackson and her three boys was windowless, the small space filled with a bunk bed, a narrow cot, and one larger bed. Donny lay on the latter, his face nearly as pale as the white pillowcase beneath him. Fern sat on the edge of the bed closest to the doorway. Another woman, a stranger to Truman, sat in a chair on the other side of the bed. He suspected her stern expression made her appear older than she was, especially with her light brown hair pulled back in a severe bun.

Fern stood. "Pastor."

"Mrs. Jackson." He tucked his Bible under his left arm, then held out his right hand to take hold of hers. "How are you?"

"I'm well. Donny, not so much."

"I'm very sorry to hear it." He motioned to the bed. "May I?"

Fern nodded. "Of course."

He sat where she had been moments before, the

covers still warm beneath him, then reached out and took one of Donny's hands between both of his. "Hello, son."

"Hello, Reverend." The boy's voice was soft and scratchy.

"I'm sorry to find you are ill again."

"Me too."

He offered a smile. "Would you mind if I prayed for you?"

Donny let his head roll slowly from side to side.

He glanced at the woman sitting primly in the chair opposite him, wondering if he should ask for an introduction. But after a momentary silence, he closed his eyes. "Heavenly Father, we come boldly into Your presence as You have invited us to do. We are not orphans left to their own devices. We are Your children, and we come to You in faith and trust to ask for healing for this boy."

Donny coughed. Softly at first. Then harder and harder, faster and faster, until it left him gasping for breath. The woman beside the bed stood at the same moment Truman stopped praying aloud. One look at her, and he moved out of her way. But his prayers continued silently as he watched her draw Donny into a seated position, bracing the boy's back with a blanket and several pillows.

"Mrs. Jackson," she said, her firm voice tinged with a Scottish brogue, "we must get this room warm. Much warmer than it is now."

- - -

Alice MacPherson scolded herself for failing to

demand more wood for the fire upon entering this ramshackle house. If the reverend hadn't arrived almost on her heels, she would have done so. Before she hardly knew what was happening, he had sat beside the boy and begun to pray.

Of course, in any normal situation, she would not have thought to interrupt a godly man's prayers. But Donny's coughing spell wasn't normal. This boy needed her help. She was a nurse, and this was what she'd trained for. She would not neglect her duty.

"Steam will help," she said as she tucked blankets around Donny's shoulders and beneath his legs. "Boil some water on the stove. Do you have the ingredients for a mustard plaster?"

Fern replied, "No, Miss MacPherson. I don't."

"Then I must get what we need."

The reverend cleared his throat. "If I can be of help . . ."

Alice straightened and met his gaze. "That would be very kind, Reverend . . .?"

"Blankenship," he supplied. "Truman Blankenship, at your service. Miss . . .?"

"MacPherson. Alice MacPherson. I am Dr. Grant's new nurse."

"Welcome to Gibeon. I did not know we were expecting you."

"No reason you should." She had little time for polite niceties. Not with a patient as ill as Donny Jackson needing seen to. She turned for her notepad and pencil. "The doctor knows what I will need, but just to be sure." She wrote quickly but neatly, then tore the paper from the book and handed it to the reverend. "Dr. Grant will have everything you need and his office is closer. But if he is not there, you can get those things at the mercantile. Be as quick as you can."

"I will hurry." He set his hat on his head and pushed through the curtained doorway, disappearing from view.

She was glad when he was gone. It freed her to go about her work. She knelt beside the bed, her skirts protecting her knees from the rough plank floor. Donny's bony chest heaved with each cough, the spasms leaving him gasping for breath. She slipped an arm behind his thin shoulders and lifted him a little higher against the pillows. "There now," she said. "Breathe slowly, lad. In through your nose, out through your mouth."

His eyes watered, and his lips were pale. Alice reached for a clean cloth from her bag and dabbed gently at his mouth and chin, wiping away the spittle. In the front parlor, the kettle rattled faintly on the stove. Fern had done as asked.

Alice rose from the floor and crossed the cramped room in two strides. At the stove in the front room, she lifted the kettle and poured steaming water into a basin, then carried it back to the bedroom. Setting the basin carefully on a stool, she bent forward, guiding the boy toward the rising vapor.

"Breathe this steam, Donny. It will ease the tightness in your chest."

He obeyed as best he could, each shallow breath catching. Alice steadied him by rubbing his back in slow, firm circles, as she'd learned to do for distressed children.

His coughs rattled less violently, though they still shook his frail body.

She glanced toward the door, willing the reverend to return with the mustard and flour. Time mattered when the lungs were so burdened. Yet she forced herself to be calm, knowing panic served neither nurse nor patient.

"Mrs. Jackson," she said over her shoulder, "fetch another blanket. The boy mustn't take a chill."

The woman went to the bunk bed in the opposite corner of the room, removing the thin blankets from both top and bottom mattresses, and Alice knew Donny's brothers would be cold tonight without them.

She looked down at her patient. "You're in my hands now, Donny Jackson, and I'll not leave you until your breathing eases. That I promise."

The child's lashes fluttered, and for the first time since she'd entered the bedroom, she saw a flicker of trust in his fever-dulled eyes.

- - -

Donny's coughing had subsided to a ragged wheeze by the time Alice heard hurried footsteps coming from outside. Moments later, Reverend Blankenship pushed back the curtain and entered, clutching a small bag in one hand.

"I brought what the doctor supplied," he said, his voice slightly winded.

"Good." Relief loosened some of the tightness in Alice's chest. She set the steaming basin aside and rose. "Come closer. I may need your help."

He obeyed without hesitation, handing her the bag. Inside were the simple ingredients she'd asked for—mustard powder, flour, and clean cloths. Alice set to work at once, mixing flour and mustard with warm water in a shallow bowl until it formed the proper paste.

"Too much mustard will blister a child's skin," she explained, more for Fern's benefit than the reverend's. "But the right amount will draw heat and loosen the phlegm." As she spread the mixture onto the cloth, a sharp, nose-prickling tang rose into the air—the dry heat of crushed mustard, pungent and medicinal, stinging the sinuses and lingering with a faintly vinegary bite. She folded the cloth neatly and carried it to the bed. Donny whimpered when she lifted his nightshirt, but she hushed him with a gentle hand. "It will help you breathe easier, lad. You'll see."

She laid the plaster on his chest and covered it with another cloth to keep the heat in. Almost at once, Donny breathed deeper than before. Alice eased him back against the pillows, smoothing his damp hair from his brow.

"Stay close, Mrs. Jackson. We'll need to check every few minutes to be certain the skin does not redden too much."

Fern nodded, her eyes filled with concern.

Alice finally allowed herself a breath of her own and looked up. The reverend had not stepped back as expected but remained nearby, his tall frame awkward in the cramped room. His eyes, however, were steady on the boy, and his hands folded as if in prayer again.

"He is in the Lord's care," he said.

Alice pressed her lips together. She had no argument against the truth of it. She believed God cared for this boy. But she also believed God helped those who helped themselves . . . as well as those who helped others. And that's what she'd come to Gibeon to do. Help others.

The British Are Coming Series
Books 1 - 6

Learn more on Robin's website.

To Enchant a Lady's Heart
To Marry an English Lord
To Capture a Mountain Man
To Reveal a Reckless Love
To Find Where She Belongs
To Fall in Love at Christmas

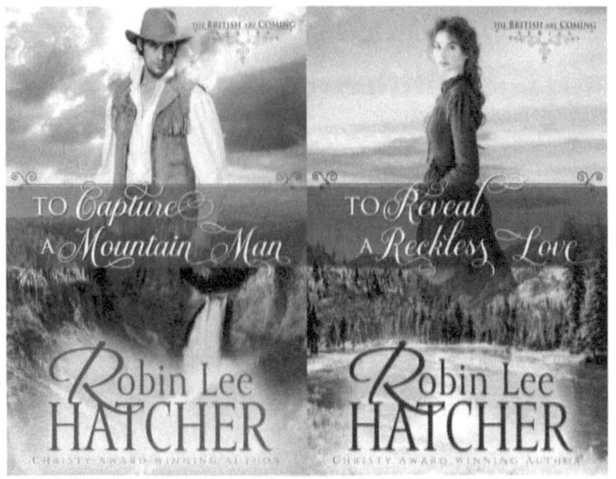

THE BRITISH ARE COMING
TO Capture A Mountain Man
Robin Lee HATCHER
CHRISTY AWARD-WINNING AUTHOR
THE BRITISH ARE COMING
TO Reveal A Reckless Love
Robin Lee HATCHER
CHRISTY AWARD-WINNING AUTHOR

THE BRITISH ARE COMING
TO Find WHERE She Belongs
Robin Lee HATCHER
CHRISTY AWARD-WINNING AUTHOR
THE BRITISH ARE COMING
TO Fall IN Love AT Christmas
Robin Lee HATCHER
CHRISTY AWARD-WINNING AUTHOR

Robin Lee Hatcher is the best-selling author of over 95 books. Her well-drawn characters and heartwarming stories of faith, courage, and love have earned her both critical acclaim and the devotion of readers. Her numerous awards include the Christy Award, the RITA® Award, Romantic Times Career Achievement Awards for Americana Romance and for Inspirational Fiction, the Carol Award, and Lifetime Achievement Awards from both Romance Writers of America® (2001) and American Christian Fiction Writers (2014).

When not writing, Robin enjoys being with her family, spending time in the beautiful Idaho outdoors, Bible art journaling, reading books that make her cry, watching romantic movies, knitting, and decorative planning. A mother and grandmother, Robin makes her home on the outskirts of Boise, sharing it with a demanding Papillon dog.

Learn more about Robin and her books and subscribe to her newsletter on her website at robinlee hatcher.com

Wagered Heart

The Perfect Life

Speak to Me of Love

Trouble in Paradise

Another Chance to Love You

Bundle of Joy

The British Are Coming

To Enchant a Lady's Heart

To Marry an English Lord

To Capture a Mountain Man

To Reveal a Reckless Love

To Find Where She Belongs

To Fall in Love at Christmas

Boulder Creek Romance

Even Forever

All She Ever Dreamed

The Coming to America Series

Dear Lady

Patterns of Love

In His Arms

Promised to Me

Where the Heart Lives Series

Belonging

Betrayal

Beloved

Books set in Kings Meadow

A Promise Kept

Love Without End

Whenever You Come Around

I Hope You Dance

Keeper of the Stars

Books set in Thunder Creek

You'll Think of Me

You're Gonna Love Me

The Sisters of Bethlehem Springs Series

A Vote of Confidence

Fit to Be Tied

A Matter of Character

Legacy of Faith series

Who I am With You

Cross My Heart

How Sweet It Is

For a full list of books, visit robinleehatcher.com